Ginger Lily

Margaret Knight

MACMILLAN CARIBBEAN WRITERS

MACMILLAN
CARIBBEAN

Macmillan Education
Between Towns Road, Oxford, OX4 3PP
A division of Macmillan Publishers Limited
Companies and representatives throughout the world

www.macmillan-caribbean.com

ISBN 1 4050 1364 8

Text © Margaret Knight 2004
Design and illustration © Macmillan Publishers Limited 2004

First published 2004

Typeset by EXPO Holdings, Malaysia
Cover design by Gary Fielder at AC Design
Cover illustration by H Ann Dodson

Dedicated
to my four children
Charles, Paul, David and Liz.

Acknowledgement
A special thanks to Frank DaSilva
who gave tremendous encouragement
to write this book.

Printed and bound in Malaysia

2008 2007 2006 2005 2004
10 9 8 7 6 5 4 3 2 1

Series Preface

Ginger Lily is the story of a love triangle between two half-brothers and the girl they both marry. The setting moves between Barbados and England, as the wilful, idealistic teenage heroine of the early chapters matures, discovering from painful experience what really matters in life's relationships. She marries against her family's wishes, bears a son, finds herself betrayed, and embarks on the lonely and difficult life of a single mother.

The Macmillan Caribbean Writers Series (MCW) is an exciting new collection of fine Caribbean writing which treats the broad range of the Caribbean experience. As well as novels and short stories the series includes poetry anthologies and collections of plays particularly suitable for Arts and Drama Festivals. There are also works of non-fiction such as an eye-witness account of life under the volatile Soufriere volcano, and another of the removal of an entire village to make way for an American base in World War II.

The series introduces unknown work by newly discovered writers, and in addition showcases new writing and favourite classics by established authors such as Michael Anthony, Jan Carew, Ian McDonald, G C H Thomas and Anthony Winkler. Writers on the list come from around the region, including Guyana, Trinidad, Tobago, Barbados, St Vincent, Bequia, Grenada, St Lucia, Dominica, Montserrat, Antigua, the Bahamas, Jamaica and Belize.

MCW was launched in 2003 at the Caribbean's premier literary event, the Calabash Festival in Jamaica. Macmillan Caribbean is also proud to be associated with the work of the Cropper Foundation in Trinidad, developing the talents of the region's most promising emerging writers, many of whom are contributors to MCW.

Judy Stone
Series Editor
Macmillan Caribbean Writers

The Macmillan Caribbean Writers Series

edited by Judy Stone

Novels:

Jeremiah, Devil of the Woods: *Martina Altmann*
Butler, Till the Final Bell: *Michael Anthony*
Such as I have: *Garfield Ellis*
The Boy from Willow Bend: *Joanne C Hillhouse*
Dancing Nude in the Moonlight: *Joanne C Hillhouse*
Ginger Lily: *Margaret Knight*
Exclusion Zone: *Graeme Knott*
The Humming-Bird Tree: *Ian McDonald*
There's No Place Like …: *Tessa McWatt*
Ruler in Hiroona: *G C H Thomas*

Plays:

Champions of the Gayelle: *(ed Judy Stone)*
　　Plays by Alwin Bully, Zeno Constance & Pat Cumper
More Champions of the Gayelle: *(ed Judy Stone)*
　　Plays by Winston Saunders, Dennis Scott & Godfrey Sealy

Stories:

Going Home, and other tales from Guyana: *Deryck M Bernard*
The Sisters, and Manco's stories: *Jan Carew*
The Annihilation of Fish and other stories: *Anthony Winkler*

1

SCHOOL in England was over, after five years. I had four credits, or what were later called 'O' levels, and one pass, with which I had to be satisfied.

Now it was back to the Caribbean. If I had not passed the pesky Cambridge School Certificate, it would have meant another year at school. Another year in England, no problem. Another year at school? A problem.

I was born on the beautiful island of Barbados. I got sent to a boarding-school in England for many reasons, which shall be made clear as time progresses.

So, here we were – my mother Ellen, my sister Gwennie and I – on our last lap through the streets of London – dear London of 1949 – in a Rickards station wagon, on our way to some obscure place called Shell Haven. Which is where we would join a Shell tanker – in fact, not just *any* old Shell tanker, but the flagship of the fleet. The mater, whom I shall refer to as Ellen from here on in, was unable to fix us up with a passage on an ordinary passenger liner, for everyone seemed to be travelling to the Caribbean. So some strings were pulled by my uncle in Barbados – who had some clout in the Shell Oil Company – and we were allotted state rooms on this flagship. *Us* ordinary personages, travelling in state rooms yet!

If you had been able to gaze out of the Rickards station wagon window with me, you would have seen all the sights that have so endeared London to my heart – Marble Arch, Leicester Square and the Moo Cow Milk Bar, the Strand, Fleet Street, St. Paul's Cathedral and the London bobby on traffic duty, to whom I blew a farewell kiss.

London – a safe haven where you could stroll nonchalantly up and down Oxford Street, Piccadilly, Park Lane and right through Hyde Park and Kensington Gardens without fear of molestation. Muggings were almost unheard of in the 1940s and '50s.

When Gwennie and I left school in Bournemouth in July 1949, we joined Ellen at a small hotel in Queensway, where we stayed for two months, until we boarded the Rickards station wagon to take us over to Shell Haven in Essex.

We arrived at Shell Haven and there was the tanker, rising and sinking slowly with the Thames tide, tied up to bollards on the dock. A long ship, she was, all newly painted, the late September afternoon sun shining on the large orange and red shell painted on her funnel. There was an oily, dockside sort of pong in the air. Not very pleasant.

The captain greeted us and showed us to our state rooms. Gwennie and I would share one and Ellen would be one deck above, next door to the Captain and his wife, who had joined him for this trip. No other passengers.

Gwennie remained in the cabin while I went back on deck to say a final farewell to dear old England. A sad moment for me. School wasn't all that bad, once you got past the first two nightmare terms. I settled in and made friends, but I don't think Gwennie ever did. She hated England and everything about it. She and I did not always get along that well. She claimed I was a rebel; I was wicked; I was deviant. A tomboy. Everything bad. Which was probably quite true. She was quiet and shy. My father, Wilfred, adored her.

Ellen? Well, bless her, she tried to keep an even balance between the two of us. It was difficult to determine who was her pet – if she had one.

"Sam?" The voice startled me. I was engrossed in watching the dock workers scurrying to and fro, preparing to cast off the good ship *Shell Queen*, with all the accompanying shouts and bangs and other loud dock noises.

It was Ellen. She put a comforting arm around my shoulders and said, "I know you're sad to leave England, but I have a feeling you'll be back some day." Small comfort. The tears welled up then and flowed freely. They washed London's grime from my cheeks and lips, and I could taste the salt.

The ship lurched, and a gap appeared between her and the dock. All kinds of ropes sprang into life along the bows and stern; there was more shouting and plenty of action. A patch of Thames water was separating me from England.

Ellen stayed with me for a while and then she went to check on Gwennie in the cabin. Gwennie was no doubt unpacking her make-up to wear to dinner that evening at the Captain's table, and sorting out her fancy dresses.

My thoughts were rudely interrupted by Gwennie. She bounced onto the deck from the open bulkhead doorway, sidled up to the rail, waved a hand in a general direction and said, "Goodbye England, and good riddance!" She whirled away and I shouted at her, "You'll miss the white cliffs of Dover." But she had already disappeared into the bowels of the ship.

What Gwennie hated most about England was the climate. She was even cold in the summer! She had also been unhappy at school, but that wasn't England's fault.

The good old English summer sun was still very much alive when we passed the white cliffs of Dover. I gazed at them and cried some more and sang the song, *White Cliffs of Dover,* made so popular by Vera Lynn.

I stayed on deck for quite a while, watching England fade away, and indeed until the sun began to set in the west, where I could see the outline of clouds on the horizon. They looked like vivid pink islands, and I thought of the little, duck-inhabited islands in the middle of the Serpentine in Hyde Park, to which I often used to row in a hired skiff.

Goodbye, dear England.

Down in the cabin, Gwennie was fussing around at the dressing-table mirror fixing her hair and finishing off the last touches to her make-up. Sometimes I wished I could be like her — petite and very feminine, with long black curly hair and an inbuilt flair for smart dressing which she certainly had not inherited from Ellen. I once heard Gwennie remark, "Mum, you look like a frump in that ghastly dress." So perhaps she inherited it from our paternal grandmother, who had died while I was an infant and was never discussed.

"Dinner is at six thirty," Gwennie announced. "The Captain came to visit and see if everything was okay, and he said that dinner is served at six thirty sharp, so you'd better get a move on and get dressed."

"I don't know what to wear."

Gwennie opened my suitcase, which Ellen had helped me pack back at the hotel. It contained a motley collection of grey school shorts, Aertex shirts, black gym shoes, white tennis shoes, socks and hundreds of other miscellaneous items. No dressy dresses. Just a standard school cotton print, Dickens & Jones, which was worn on evenings in the summer.

"Where's that lovely pink dress with the black lace that Mum bought for you at C & A., which she said would be ideal to wear at dinner on board?"

"In the trunk. In the hold."

"*What?* I don't believe it!"

Just then, Ellen entered the cabin. "Is this what you're looking for?" She fluttered the pink and black dress in her hands. She had a wicked smile on her face when she looked at me and said, "I saw you put that in the trunk, so I took it out and put it in my suitcase. Sam, you really are the limit. What did you intend to wear to dinner?"

"What's wrong with this skirt and a clean Aertex shirt?"

Gwennie and Ellen exchanged looks and sighs.

Dinner was in the small dining saloon. There was a long table at which sat the Captain, his wife and about four officers. I liked the Captain. He had a jolly face with greying hair and bushy eyebrows and twinkling blue eyes. He and his wife were Dutch but they both spoke English fluently.

Captain and officers all rose from their seats when Ellen, Gwennie and I joined them at the table, and a dashingly handsome steward whose nickname was Tiger, I discovered, pulled out our chairs.

The food? I'd never seen anything like it. Scrumptious. You spend five years in an English boarding-school, you get used to kippers for breakfast, bully beef, spuds, sloshy cabbage and foul-tasting brussels sprouts for lunch, and mushy rhubarb for dessert. So imagine Gwennie and I going to town on the Scandinavian hors d'oeuvres, followed by soup, then roast beef, baby potatoes, green vegetables and a side salad. Heaven!

At first there was no sign of sea-sickness. The English Channel was calm. They all said, "Wait until we reach the Bay of Biscay." Yes, we knew from past experience!

There was this officer who kept eyeing Gwennie, and she kept flickering her eyelashes at him. Occasionally the corners of their mouths twitched in a shy smile. I think the Captain had observed these coy but come-hither exchanges, because I saw him exchange a rather knowing smile with his wife.

Ellen appeared not to notice anything because she was busy chatting with the Captain's wife. When Ellen started chatting she sometimes found it difficult to find a cut-off point, especially if Wilfred wasn't around.

"And vhat vill your two lovely daughters do now that they are finished school, Mrs Kinley?" asked the Captain's wife.

Ellen smiled proudly at Gwennie. "Well, Gwennie has just completed a secretarial course at St James's Secretarial College in London and I think she's rather keen to work in a bank. They pay well, you know." Then she glanced at me. She looked embarrassed. "Samantha has not quite decided what she wants to do. She was very keen to join the WRNS, but Wilfred, my husband, was not agreeable."

That was true enough. Wilfred and Ellen had visited Bournemouth a few times and taken Gwennie and me out for weekend sprees.

The inevitable question always arose. What did I wish to do when I left school? All kinds of hair-brained schemes entered my head, but my main ambition was to join the Women's Royal Naval Service. "Absolutely and definitely not," Wilfred had insisted, though God only knew why. What was wrong with being a WREN?

"But Dad, that is what I would like to do. Is this my life, or is this my life?"

"Don't be rude, Samantha. I simply do not wish any of my daughters to be in the military. Can't you be a secretary like Gwennie, or do medicine like me?"

"Huh! A doctor, when I gave up Latin and Science in Fourth Form? Come on, Dad, you know I can't do medicine."

"Well, how about nursing then?" On and on went the battle royal, which always ended in a stalemate.

Wilfred was no doubt waiting in Barbados to pounce on me once more, as soon as we set foot on shore at Bridgetown. I was in a quandary. I would probably end up as a receptionist in his office, taking down patients' boring details.

Tiger winked at me and I winked back. No one noticed; Ellen was still chatting away to Mrs Captain, and the Captain was chatting up Gwennie.

And so to sleep, lulled by the gentle rolling of the *Shell Queen,* ploughing her way steadily towards the Atlantic, soon to be passing through the dreaded Bay of Biscay.

Anticlimax. The Bay of Biscay was like a duck pond. Unbelievable, said the Captain. Incredible, said the young officer who fancied Gwennie. His name was Richard and he was Apprentice Third Mate.

At dinner on the fourth night out and well into the Atlantic, just passing the Azores, the Captain announced that a hurricane was heading our way. Not a severe one, but nevertheless we could expect some rough weather. Tankers, he informed us, were low in the water – lower when they were full of oil on the way back up north from Curacao – but we were loaded with ballast. Some consolation when you knew a hurricane was approaching.

The hurricane hit the next day. *Shell Queen* danced and skipped, rocked, rolled and pitched. At one point she almost turned fully around and headed back to Blighty.

Gwennie was puking all over the bathroom and on the deck above, Ellen was puking all over the state room. I got worried about her, so I fought my way up the companionway and went to help her. I offered to stay in the cabin with her until the weather cleared up or she stopped puking, whichever was first. I assured her that Richard was taking care of Gwennie.

Tiger brought up my suitcase and I settled into Ellen's cabin. Somehow, I avoided the *mal-de-mer*, and so managed to look after Ellen.

When the hurricane was over and Ellen regained her strength, she suggested I remain with her for the rest of the voyage. No point in lugging the suitcase back down again. I suspected it was something more than that. She had observed the growing relationship between Richard and Gwennie, and she liked Richard.

Day Seven and the weather was beautiful. The sun was shining, somewhat glaringly, on the Atlantic, and every now and then huge clumps of moss floated past the bows, and flying fish flew away from the sides of the ship like tiny rockets. Richard said the moss was from the Sargasso Sea.

Three days later we arrived in Curacao where we spent two days at the Piscadera Beach Club before flying on to Trinidad, via Caracas.

After breakfast on the day before we were due to arrive in Curacao, I found Richard painting some rails on deck. Good-looking bloke was Richard. Blond hair with a cowlick that graced his wide forehead. Blue eyes and a mischievous smile, which he now bestowed upon me. "Morning. Bet you'll be glad to be on land tomorrow."

I shrugged. "I guess. This trip hasn't been too bad. We've had some fun; better than if we'd been on a passenger ship with all the frills and fancies."

Richard cocked his head and smiled. "Wouldn't have thought you'd have thought that, you being so lively and all."

He stopped painting. "The Old Man will kill me if he sees me talking instead of working, but to hell with it! Gwennie tells me you enjoyed boarding-school. I find that incredible."

It was not up to me to go into detail about Gwennie's likes and dislikes, because I think they went pretty deep and had their roots embroiled in Wilfred's background, which was somewhat chequered if we could believe what a cousin had revealed to us.

I often wondered if she accepted who she was, or if she was in total denial and so assumed aloofness as a mask. She seemed to find it difficult to get along with people as a general rule, therefore I was quite surprised when she struck up a friendship with Richard at such an early stage. She had never adjusted to boarding-school and all that went along with it – the confinement, the teasing and cattiness of some of the girls, the mandatory games such as lacrosse and netball in the winter and tennis and rounders in the summer. Gwennie hated outdoor games.

For two young girls to be whisked away from a tiny Caribbean island and dumped down in a boarding-school in an ultra-conservative place like Bournemouth was, to say the least, upsetting.

Wilfred was a doctor and a very strict disciplinarian, which is fine – so long as it's coupled with some love. I am not sure that Wilfred was capable of love – or at least of showing it. You followed the rules which he laid down, and God help you if you disobeyed them. This was how he had been brought up in the Victorian era, and that was that. His father had been a captain in the British Army, based in Barbados. The colonial era. My grandfather had shocked all the middle and upper class whites in the island, not to mention the Army from which he was kicked out, by marrying a mulatto lady. And there was the crux of the matter. Again, this was according to a relative. "*Shame and scandal in de family!*"

When Wilfred and his brother, Walter, were growing up, they were obviously subject to much rejection and ostracism from all quarters. Snobbery was equally as common in Barbados, it being such a small, tight-knit community, as it was in Olde England. Wilfred and Walter did not attend the island's prestigious boys' public school, Harrison College, for the very same reason. Their father was well-off, having inherited money from his father, who had been one of those hated 'rich white planters', and he had engaged the services of a top class private tutor for his two sons. He had no intention of exposing them to the inevitable insults they would have suffered at a public school.

The trials and tribulations of the aforesaid matters seemed to slide off Walter like water off a duck's back. He paid no attention to the slurs and sly innuendos – he had long since decided that he was going to make a success of his life and he would override the obstacles in his way. Which is exactly what he did. By the age of forty-five, he was a company director and he married a Spanish lady from Venezuela and sailed through life.

Not so Wilfred. He bore a heavy chip on his shoulder. His father pulled his pockets and sent him off to Canada to study medicine. He returned to Barbados a doctor and married into a very refined family, with their roots in Scotland, and got on with his life. But he never forgave his father for marrying a 'coloured' lady. I often wondered if he loved his mother. He never talked of her, and as for asking questions, better you went and hanged yourself from a mahogany tree.

Richard brought me back from my reminiscences. He was asking how come I liked boarding-school.

"Oh, I didn't always like it, you know. I hated it at first. I hated the cold in winter and I hated the confinement. I had been accustomed to so much freedom in Barbados. When I wasn't swimming in the sea, or on the beach playing around, I was climbing a tree. I guess Gwennie has told you I am somewhat of a tomboy. I suppose I really started to settle in at school in my second year. I had begun to make friends, and the girls had stopped teasing me and calling me a 'colonial' and asking me if I wore a grass skirt in Barbados. When they asked me that, I replied, 'Heavens, no. I wore *nothing*.' That shut them up. After that things were pretty cool for me, and at one point I got a bit swell-headed because I had become the school's swimming champion, and eventually the tennis vice-captain – I had a wicked serve. So, I had 'arrived'. I was happy then. Story of my life so far, Richard."

Gwennie appeared at that moment, wearing a cute little sun top and a pair of shorts. She looked fresh and smelled of flowery perfume. She gave me a forbidding look, "hands off my man" sort of thing, and I said lamely, "Oh, I was just exchanging boarding-school views with Richard."

I sauntered off to look for Ellen.

2

W E hadn't really seen much of Curacao, being confined, so to speak, at Piscadera Bay, but we had visited Willemstadt which was quaint with Dutch colonial-style buildings, but rather smelly. Curacao had one thing going for it at that time – oil. And so on to Trinidad which fascinated and yet depressed me. Port of Spain was a mass of confusion with a tremendously cosmopolitan population. East Indians, negroes, whites and mulattos, Portuguese originally from Brazil, Spanish from Venezuela, and 'Douglas' who are half-Indian, half-negro. The city smelled of Indian *roti* and many other spicy foods. I always feel somewhat claustrophobic in Port of Spain, which is surrounded by mountains. It is the land of the humming-bird, and the land of steelband, calypso and carnival. It is sticky, hot and humid, and traffic buzzes around in every direction, car horns blaring, and people shouting at one another across the busy streets.

An East Indian will meet you at the top of Frederick Street, selling a silver bracelet for ten dollars, and by the time you reach the bottom of Frederick Street, you have beaten him down to two dollars. Mind you, the silver filigree bracelet will tarnish after a few wearings on your sweaty wrist.

We were spending one night in a guest-house in St Anne's, round by Queen's Park. The Queen's Park Hotel was the posh one, but I guess Wilfred was a bit strapped for cash after dishing out all that money on his two brats in Bournemouth.

First thing I had to do in the bedroom after plunking the old suitcase down in a corner, was to search the entire room – under the bed, pull back the covers, in the closet, in the bathroom, under chairs and dressing table – in the ghastly event that I should find a tarantula spider. Trinidad is full of them. A Trinidadian whom I met on the ship going to England in 1945 told me so, and he should know.

All night, as I lay tossing and turning, I imagined things crawling on me in bed. I was glad to see the light of day and to be off to the docks to board the Canadian steamship *Lady Rodney* for the last leg of our journey. No state rooms, just a four-berth cabin, but we got entertained that night in the finely decorated dining saloon by a full orchestra, which played some of my favourite music – Glenn Miller stuff.

Three days later, after making stops at Grenada and St Vincent, we arrived in Carlisle Bay, Bridgetown.

I got up at the crack of dawn when we were still about an hour away from dropping anchor, and I watched the outline of Barbados growing closer and larger in the early morning light. I could see the hills of St George and Shop Hill, St Thomas, and the twinkling lights of Bridgetown, growing ever dimmer as the morning sun peeped over the hills.

I had very mixed feelings. When I had left Barbados, all those years ago, I had been distraught, to say the least. Neither Gwennie nor I knew what we were going to. The image of England imprinted on our minds was that of a cold, unfriendly country, recovering from the devastation of war. All the English people we had met on the island were snooty and unfriendly.

Wilfred and Ellen had a few English friends, but they all seemed to be single men or women, or married couples with no children. When Wilfred had enquired of them about boarding-schools in England, one of them had suggested Roedean and another one suggested Cheltenham Ladies College. However, a third one vetoed both of those schools and suggested a much smaller one in Bournemouth. "The girls won't feel so overwhelmed," he had declared. Thank God for that bloke.

Gwennie sneaked up behind me as I stood at the rail, and I jumped when she spoke. "Look at it! Will you just look at Bimshire!"

I'm not quite sure how Barbados got nicknamed 'Bimshire', but it is thought that some half-wit said it was like England and that perhaps one of the shires had separated and floated down the Atlantic.

"God, what a sight for sore eyes," she went on. "Look at the green hillsides, the dazzling white beaches, the coconut palms. I can't wait to get on my swimsuit and plunge into that blue Caribbean sea."

She was right. It was a sight for sore eyes.

A tender was approaching the ship, which had dropped anchor with much rumbling and groaning from the winch in the bows, and a great big plop and splash. Ellen joined Gwennie and I on deck. She was craning her neck to see into the tender. Looking for Wilfred. He was there all right – cigarette in his mouth and all. He was a rather short, stocky man, and like the Captain of the *Shell Queen*, he had rather bushy eyebrows and a hooked nose.

The tender parked itself off by the gangway and Wilfred came on board. Hugs and kisses and smiles all round. Not normally an affectionate man, but this was a special occasion. Ellen was glowing all over.

We were finally home, in beautiful Barbados. I had forgotten how hot it was, especially in October.

Wilfred had breakfast on board with us and then we all trooped down the gangway and into the little launch that was bobbing up and down beside the bottom step of the gangway.

While Gwennie and I had been at school in England, learning how to say "How now brown cow" properly, Wilfred had been busying himself in Barbados running around looking for a house on the beach to buy. He found one on the West Coast. A spacious four-bedroom bungalow with two bathrooms. A long driveway lined by mahogany trees led up to the front patio; a huge lawn to the east of the house was bordered by a display of various flowering shrubs. To the west, the glorious white expanse of beach and the glittering blue Caribbean Sea. To the north of the house were four acres of woods made up of mahogany, manchineel, whitewood, cordia, casuarinas, sea grapes and coconut palms, all swaying in the breeze from the north-east trade winds.

Two servants met us at the front door, Kellman the butler-cum-handyman, and Meg, the cook, dressed in a light blue frock with a white apron and white cap on her head. Both Kellman and Meg wore huge smiles on their dark faces, and I was overjoyed to see my darling Meg again. How I had missed her. She was fat and jolly with a most comfortable lap, and two huge boobs upon which, as a young child, I had often rested my head, thumb in mouth, and gone off to sleep.

It was hot and humid and already thunderheads were building over towards the south, and if we didn't hurry up and dash down to the beach to have a quick swim, we would likely get caught in a storm. So Gwennie and I rushed inside, tore open suitcases, found swimsuits and were down on the beach in minutes, leaving Ellen and Wilfred to kiss and hug – if ever they did that – and make up for their absence from each other.

Ellen was quite an affectionate person, particularly with her brothers and sisters, upon whom she could lavish affection and have it returned. She was born at the turn of the twentieth century into a rather large family who had lived most of their lives on various plantations, mostly in the parish of St Thomas. Her hair was mouse-brown and to a certain extent she resembled the Hollywood movie star, June Allison. Her brow was wrinkled and her blue eyes twinkled when she smiled. She was a 'do-er'; always doing something – sewing dresses for Gwennie and me, or for our dolls, knitting in the 1940s for the war effort, an avid churchgoer and a member of the Mother's Union and the Fellowship of Marriage. Although rather quiet, she was jovial at times, with a great sense of humour when let loose amongst her siblings.

Wilfred was the opposite. Quiet and often withdrawn. He possessed what I thought was rather a warped sense of humour. He loved to make fun of people's idiosyncrasies. He made the most fabulous rum cocktails which everyone called 'Wilfred's brew'.

We had an enjoyable swim, Gwennie and I, but it was rather short, because of the looming thunderheads and the rain, which had begun to spatter.

Wilfred and Ellen were sitting in the wide veranda overlooking the beach, sipping drinks, when Gwennie and I joined them. The cocktail shaker on a side table contained 'egg flips', as Wilfred called them. Rum-based eggnogs with lots of nutmeg floating on the top. Delicious after a swim.

I hate thunderstorms, but we hadn't been sitting in the veranda for more than ten minutes before we heard the first rumble of thunder and the rain was sweeping in sheets across the sea, so we abandoned the veranda and moved into the drawing room, which contained all of the furniture that we had left at the old house before sailing for England. It looked good in this setting, for the old house had been one of the older type Barbadian homes, with shuttered doors and windows and storm shutters on inside doors. It had also had a chimney on the kitchen roof, from which curled the smoke from the wood and coal stove used in days gone by.

Wilfred and Ellen were discussing politics. Wilfred sometimes got quite hot under the collar when discussing this subject. He appeared to have little use for Mr Grantley Adams, who had successfully initiated the famous 1937 riots, when, to put it in a nutshell, he incited sugar workers and other agricultural labourers into rioting against ridiculously low wages. Ironically, over thirty black people were killed – many by black policemen under the supervision of a white police commissioner – and no whites sustained injuries.

I was just coming up to six years old and Gwennie was eight when, on July 26th, we witnessed the rumblings of the riots. I hadn't a clue what it was all about, except that the names on everyone's lips were Grantley Adams and Clement Payne. It bothered me little, and in fact I began to liken it in my mind to a Red Indian-cowboy rootin' tootin' shootout.

I became apprehensive, however, when I heard Ellen and Wilfred discussing what would be the likely outcome. The black people would be swiftly "put in their places" by the police, and some would no doubt die. That did bother me because I dearly loved Meg and I had a certain amount of affection for Kellman, although he and I were many times at loggerheads, since he was always threatening to "tell the master or mistress" what I had done, and one such crime was playing with black children on the beach. That was a definite no-no. Kellman often carried out his threats and I got my bare bum whacked by Wilfred with a tamarind twig.

Years later, when reading about pornography and masochistic tendencies, I found it difficult to associate bum lashings with pleasure, sexual or otherwise. That tamarind twig stung, and was distinctly *unpleasant*.

The first night of the riots was particularly painful for me. The house was completely barred up, with storm shutters in place, and Wilfred walked up and down, revolver in hand, all night. Distant gun shots could be heard from time to time throughout the night. I was fearful for Meg and I thought about her all night. I worried that she might be shot or injured in some way.

A few days later, everything was back to normal. Meg was safe and so was Kellman. The labourers got what they asked for – higher wages and better conditions, because the British

Government in its infinite wisdom and upon advice from the
Colonial Secretary, had intervened.

Our new home had a name. Originally called Casa Linda, Ellen
changed it to Ginger Lily. Ellen had a passion for lilies, she planted
them all over the place. Some in a lily pond, along with hyacinths.
She planted amaryllis lilies all along the walkway to the beach.
Ginger lilies lined the driveway, in between the mahogany trees,
and at the northern end of the lawn. The ginger lilies, some pink
and some red, seemed to thrive all year round.

To the north of the house and rather subtly hidden, Wilfred had
had his office and waiting room built, and he had lots of patients
from the surrounding areas. He knew his medical stuff and was a
surprisingly sympathetic doctor.

A few days after we returned and having just about settled in, I
was figuring it was about time I had a little chat with Wilfred
because I didn't know where I was going or what I was doing.
Gwennie and Ellen were all busy making plans for Gwennie's
wedding to Richard. The lovebirds had been in constant touch
and had decided to tie the knot as soon as Richard could get leave
from the Shell Company. They told me I had to be chief brides-
maid. Not something I was wild about.

Wilfred was in his office sipping tea, having just seen his last
patient. I knocked on the door and he yelled, "Come in."

The office had a desk and two chairs, a couch with a curtain
around it, a washbasin and two or three white enamel tables with
bowls and other medical paraphernalia, including a microscope,
cluttering them. Over on one wall were shelves with all kinds of
labelled bottles stacked on them.

Wilfred's spectacles were perched on the end of his nose and he
dipped his head to look at me.

"Hi, dad. Could I talk to you?"

He consulted his watch. "Yes, I've finished for the day, and I was
just going to go and take a rest, but what's on your mind?"

"Well, I've been thinking. I can't loaf around Barbados doing
nothing all day. I mean, it's wonderful to be back home and
spending half the day in the sea, but for how long?"

"Well, why not just take it easy for a month or two at least, and
start thinking about what you would like to do eventually. As a

matter of fact, I have been thinking too. I wondered if you might be interested in helping me in the office. You could either do a secretarial course, or I could teach you to do a few minor tests, and that way you would gain a little medical experience."

"Tests? What kind of tests?"

He cleared his throat. "Oh, just urine, and perhaps blood haemoglobin, that sort of thing."

Me – testing pee. I'd just completed a reasonable education and all my father could think about for me to do was testing pee.

"Could I think about it?"

"Of course. Take your time." I thought he was finished with me because he rose from his swivel chair and shoved his spectacles back on his green eyes. But he said, "On the other hand, you might like to consider returning to England after a while, and doing something over there. I have to tell you that I do not hold out much hope for this island, the way things are going. Ten, maybe fifteen years from now this will be no place for white people, mark my words. You can see for yourself how uppity the negroes ..."

"Dad, please ..."

He gave me a scornful look. "As I was saying, the black people – if that suits you better – have become uppity. They are getting ready to take over, and when they do, they will destroy everything that has been achieved in Barbados. Wherever they go in this world, they destroy. They never contribute a damn thing to any society."

I did not wish to listen to his diatribe, because I knew what would follow – *That damned man Adams, he caused all of this; a white man put him in the position he is in today; the blacks have lost all respect for white people; one of these days you might even see a white Bajan marrying a black one; I don't know where it will all end,* on and on he would go. So I quickly said, "I may just think about returning to England, but not for those reasons," and I walked out.

3

CHRISTMAS was upon us. After some heavy rainfall accompanied by ear-shattering thunderstorms throughout September, October and November, the lawn was green and the garden was beautiful with the poinsettias and snow-on-the-mountain all in full bloom.

Ellen was busy at the sewing machine every day, making a fancy dress for me to wear to the coming out, or launching, or whatever they called it, of her two daughters, at the annual Coming Out Ball at the Marine Hotel. This was where I was supposed to meet my Mr Right, Gwennie having already met hers. She was still going to the wretched Ball, but our cousin was to be her chaperone, seeing as how she was engaged and all.

Wilfred, of course, was in his element. He was convinced that I would meet Mr Right from the Right family, get engaged and married and have all the Right children (all white, of course), who would eventually leave the island for boarding-school in England. And who knows, one of them might even marry a Sir Somebody, or better yet a Duke or an Earl. Poor Wilfred.

Unfortunately, I had news for him. I had no intention whatsoever of finding a Mr Right, let alone marrying him. I had, in fact, spied a very handsome young man who lived just up the road in a little fishing village called Boston Bay. He was tall with curly black hair, very expressive eyes and a wide mouth that spread a smile all over his face. He was brown-skinned. He cycled past our house quite often on his way to Holetown. I knew this, because one day I found a poor wounded wood dove in the road and just as I was picking it up, he cycled by. He stopped the bicycle and grinned at me. I said, "Hi."

"What are you going to do with that bird?" he asked.

"Take it inside and look after it until it is well enough to fly again."

"It will die."

"Oh, thanks. Thanks a whole heap for your encouraging words."

He sped off on his bicycle without another word. I looked at the bird and said, "Well, how do you like that cheeky bugger, bird?"

Sad to say, the cheeky bugger was right. The little bird died about a week later, although both Ellen and I had tried our best to save it.

Ellen had finished the dress for the pesky Coming Out Ball. She had bought the material at Selfridges before we left England. I had to admit it was beautiful. White background with a soft flowered pattern, and long skirt reaching to just below the ankles. I felt like Cinderella. Ellen was making me try it on in front of the long mirror and I was fidgeting and shifting from foot to foot.

"Hold still, will you," exclaimed an exasperated Ellen.

"It itches and tickles."

"Of course it does. New material always does. Now there you are, turn around and have a look."

I looked. For once I looked like a lady. I guess Ellen was satisfied. She made me take it off carefully and I got stuck with pins. I exited her sewing room in a hurry.

Just then the phone rang. I answered it. Hesitation at the other end, then, a soft-spoken male voice stuttered, "May I speak to … uh … Sam, please?"

Something familiar about that voice. "Samantha speaking."

"Oh, sorry. Don't they call you 'Sam' any more?"

The voice was definitely familiar. "Yes, they do. But – excuse me, who wants to know?"

"Uh … Tony. Tony Brownfield. Remember me?"

I did. Grew up with Tony and his sister, Julie. They had lived a few houses away from us, when we had lived in that white enclave known as Strathmore in St Michael. That was before Gwennie and I got shipped off to England.

Strathmore was a residential area, laid out in avenues with a tennis club somewhere in the middle, where everyone went to play tennis and drink rum punches. Black people were not allowed to walk through Strathmore unless they were domestic servants working at the houses. A proper little South Africa. The houses were practically identical. All two-storey, with large drawing room, dining room, breakfast room, closed-in verandah, kitchen downstairs, and three or four bedrooms and one bathroom upstairs.

Tony Brownfield. Fancy that. He and I used to ride our bicycles like crazy up and down the avenues, singing at the tops of our voices and causing the little old ladies who lived in some of the houses to appear at their windows and shout threats at us.

Wilfred would have punished me for sure, had he known, and Tony's father, who had a terrible temper and was often somewhat inebriated, would have got out the leather strap out and tanned Tony's hide.

"Tony Brownfield! Well, blow me down. How are you? *Que pasa?*"

Tony laughed. "Ah, so you remember our favourite Spanish phrase. I heard you were back from England and that your Dad bought a beautiful bungalow on the beach in St James. Do you like it?"

"It's smashing. I love it. It's good to be back home, and best of all to be able to run down the beach and into the sea. It's heavenly. But I miss England. I miss London and the Underground trains and Oxford Circus and browsing around in Foyles Bookstore, and feeding the ducks in the Serpentine in Hyde Park, and – oh, just everything about London."

"Yeah. Well, listen. Are you going to be coming out at the Marine? And if so, could I be your escort?"

Uh-oh, I thought. Wilfred's been at it. I'll bet he's been talking to Mr Brownfield, scheming to get Tony and I together. If that's the case, I simply won't go.

"Tony, why are you asking me? Did your father and Wilfred scheme this together?"

An explosion on the phone. "Jesus, Sam, do you think I'm still a child? I left school this year. I am nineteen and I am totally independent, except that Dad took me into his business for six months before I enter university in Canada. I'm sort of apprenticing with the old man, if you will. He can't rule my life. If you don't wish to go with me, say so."

A right twit I am. I apologised. "I'm sorry, Tony. I just thought … well, you know Wilfred. Of course I would love to go to the Ball with you. Mum has just made me a gorgeous dress, and I'm all ready."

We talked some more and reminisced a bit on days gone by, and then we said *hasta la vista* and rang off.

The Marine Hotel was its splendiferous self, all glittering with coloured lights and balloons and decorations all over the dance floor. People were arriving and car doors were slamming as debutantes stepped out, some on their fathers' arms, others with their escorts.

Tony looked magnificent in his tuxedo and bow tie and all. If he had been good-looking in his childhood, he was now ruggedly handsome. A sort of Clark Gable-without-the-moustache ruggedness. Light brown hair, light brown eyes with golden flecks, and a dimple in his chin. I felt proud to be escorted by him, and I noticed many girls giving him the eye.

Gwennie looked beautiful in a powder blue full-length dress with frills and ruffles and whatnot, but her face wore a slightly sad look. She was missing Richard.

They corresponded frequently, and although a date had not yet been set for their forthcoming marriage, we all knew it would be shortly after the New Year. Richard had left Shell and was with the Harrison Line, plying the Caribbean route. He was awaiting their permission for leave to get hitched.

Gwennie dangled on our cousin Ian's arm, as they made their way up the steps and into the ballroom. Wilfred glowed like a glow-worm. He found us a table up front close to the bandstand. The music was by Percy Green's orchestra, which was considered the best dance-band in the island at that time.

Wilfred ordered drinks and we sat and gazed around at people. Ellen and Wilfred kept waving and nodding at people they knew. Gwennie and I had lost touch with many of our old friends and it was kind of exciting seeing and recognising them again. Faces do not change that much in four or five years but hairstyles certainly do.

Wilfred suddenly sat bolt upright and leaned across the table, trying to whisper but not quite managing it, to Ellen. "Look at them!" he exclaimed, inclining his head towards a couple who were just seating themselves at a table. "See what this island is coming to? They would never have been able to buy tickets to this Ball before."

The couple he referred to were coloured, but so pale it was difficult to distinguish them from whites. A lot of white people sitting at tables nearby waved to them and greeted them with smiles. I sighed. My dad had a problem.

The band started playing a Glenn Miller medley. Tony got up and asked me to dance. And Wilfred grabbed Gwennie before Ian could. Protocol, I believe it's called.

Tony was a good dancer, but a peculiar thing happened to me when I looked at him, and it sent a shiver down my spine. Instead of seeing Tony's face, I saw the face of the brown-skinned bloke from Boston Bay, who cycled to Holetown every day. Catastrophe in the making!

Tony held me off a bit and looked at me kind of oddly. "Why did you look at me like that?" he enquired.

I felt like a fool. I didn't know what the hell to say. Why had that happened? I shrugged. "Gosh, Tony, I'm sorry. I guess I was … ah … admiring how handsome and grown-up you look."

"Why, thank you, Sam. I beat you to it though; I was admiring you all evening!"

I inclined my head and murmured a pitiful thank you, which failed to sound genuine.

"I missed you, Sam." This said with a little hand-squeezing.

I did not reply because in all honesty, if I echoed his sentiments I would be lying. It was good seeing him again and I felt proud to be with him, but I could not shake off the niggling thoughts of the Boston Bay boy that persisted in invading my mind. Why? I kept asking myself, as if that would help.

When we got back to the table, Ellen and Wilfred were excitedly discussing a couple who were dancing. The young man was Our Roy – better known to his adoring Mum as 'my little carrot'. He had red hair and a lilywhite skin, and people said he was a pansy boy. So, according to Wilfred, what the heck was he doing at a Debutante Ball with a girl in tow!

"Just look at him!" exclaimed Wilfred, leaning closer to Ellen. "Isn't he just too much? He even dances like a girl."

Ellen said, "Joyce tells me she is so proud of her 'little carrot' because he has recently returned from England, having done a course on antiques, and he is going to set up an antique business along with a young man from Martinique."

"Probably a faggot like him," declared Wilfred.

"Wilfred, keep your voice down. The music has stopped. Furthermore, Roy is a perfect gentleman. Notice how he always jumps up from the table when people come over to talk to Joyce? His late departed father would be very proud."

I had always liked Roy so I excused myself and sauntered over to Joyce and Roy's table. Roy sprang up like a young buck, and came to give me a hug and a kiss. "Good Lord – Samantha! My, my, but you're so grown up and delightfully pretty. *Do* join us. Mums, you remember Sam, don't you?"

Joyce, her face almost a mask with far too much make-up, nodded her head vigorously and extended a hand upon which hung a few jangling gold bracelets.

"Of course I do. Sit down, Sam, and tell us all your juicy bits and pieces. I see you're with Tony." Her thickly pencilled eyebrows jumped up and down, insinuating a lot. I stole a furtive glance across at our table and observed that Wilfred was stealing furtive glances across at us.

I smiled at Joyce. "Nothing serious, Mrs Jermaine, I assure you."

"Oh, Sam, please call me Joyce. You're not a child now."

"She certainly isn't, and oh, look at her deportment," piped up Our Roy, clapping his delicate hands together. "That's what boarding school does for you. I wish I had known you were coming out this year – I would have been *so happy* to have escorted you."

I remembered the pretty girl he had been dancing with. "But, where is your belle? Did I not see you dancing just now?"

Joyce and Roy exchanged glances. "*I* am his belle, Sam," Joyce replied.

"Let me explain, Mums. Sam, I am rather distressed because most of the young ladies these days appear to be after two things – money and sex. So I opted to escort my mother. The one I made the mistake of dancing with – she's a good-looking girl, but ..."

"She comes from nothing," cut in Joyce.

"Mums, *please*. She was pushing herself too close to me and sort of rubbing up against me. You know what I mean, Sam."

It was all I could do not to laugh out loud, but you never know with homosexuals how they will react to certain emotions, so I inclined my head and gave a tactful smile, like they taught me to do at boarding-school.

I sat with them for a while, then made my excuses when I saw Tony coming towards our table. He wanted to dance.

4

A tour around Gwennie's boudoir was an experience. It was pretty with frilly lace curtains and a bed with a fancy canopy. Gwennie did it herself. She was working at Barclays Bank in Bridgetown so she got a good salary and she loved pretty things. When we were children, she played with beautiful dolls for which Ellen made the clothes on her Singer machine, while I climbed trees and sped around Strathmore on my bicycle.

I knocked on Gwennie's door and opened it a crack. "Can I come in?"

"Sure, Sam. I'm just polishing my fingernails. Want to do yours?"

I laughed. "Fingernails? You must be joking – I don't have any. I bite them!"

"Sign of nervousness, Sam. I thought you had outgrown biting your nails."

"Nah. Wish I could." I sat in her rocking chair. "Is this an antique? Roy would love it for his upcoming antique business."

"It is indeed an antique, and Our Roy is definitely not going to get it. It had belonged to Granny – don't you remember? You can have it when I get married, but not to sell to Roy!"

"I'm thinking of working with Roy when he opens his shop. We discussed it the other night at the Ball. He said he would be delighted to have me come and help him."

"Dad won't be pleased. He is glad of your help in his surgery, I believe."

I had started working with Wilfred, for which he paid me the 'handsome' sum of $60.00 a month. Gwennie got $100.00 a month plus bonuses and other perks at the Bank. While she was 'balancing' books, I was balancing things on scales, testing pee and cleaning bottles of all kinds of pharmaceutical things, many of which were acids.

"Yeah, well. I'm kinda fed up testing pee now. I like haemotology but that's a bit advanced for me. A dreadful old man sneaked up behind me one day when I was busy dipping litmus paper in someone's pee, and startled me. 'I hope that's not my piss you're examining,' says he. 'It's a terrible colour.' I told him it was not his, and then he had the audacity to ask me whose it was!"

Gwennie giggled. "Why did he want to know that?"

"Malicious old bugger. He said he wanted to know so as he could avoid the person who obviously had a terrible disease." We both had a good laugh.

I shifted in the rocker. "Gwennie, I want to ask you a few questions."

"Shoot."

"First of all, what's the real story on Dad's mother – our esteemed-but-never-talked-about grandmother?"

"Sam, we've been through this before. I don't really know any more than you do, and you know that Dad and Mum will not discuss it. All I know is that she was coloured, light-skinned. Half-caste, in other words. But Sam, most so-called whites in Barbados come from a similar background, so what's your beef?"

"*My* beef? Not my beef, Gwennie. Wilfred's beef, you mean. I am more interested to know if we have family on our grandmother's side, and if so, who and where are they. That's what I would like to know."

"Why?"

"Why what? Why do I wish to know who they are? Jesus, Gwennie, they're *family* – whoever they are. I would like to meet them."

"*What?* Sam, I wouldn't advise that. If Dad found out he would do his bloody nut!"

"Well then, let him. Don't you think he had a duty to tell us about our background? *All of it?* He concentrates on his father's side of the family and how they originated from the bloody landed gentry in Hampshire and all that crap, and he takes delight in showing off the family crest. You know something? Our old man has a problem, Gwennie."

"Well, Sam, it's his problem. Not ours. Leave things be. We're not suffering. We're happy, we enjoy the good things in life, and … by the way, aren't you and Tony getting together again?"

I laughed and shrugged. "Nicely done, Gwennie. Sidetrack Sam and she'll shut up about Wilfred. Okay. Tony? Yes, he phones me and we're going to movies on Saturday night and probably to Club

Morgan after that but ..." I shrugged. I was thinking about the Boston Bay boy. Don't ask me why.

Gwennie gave me a quizzical look. "You have a problem with Tony? He's a very nice young man, Sam. You would do well to stick with him. He's got a level head on those broad shoulders, and he's going to have money one day."

I rocked forward and remained suspended. "*Shit*, Gwennie, money, money, money! That's all people seem to think about." Rocking chairs have a tendency to do their own thing and back it went, which somewhat diminished my emphasis, so I stood up and kicked the rocking chair.

"Temper, temper! And don't swear. What's so bad about thinking of money? We all need it! So, what are the other questions?"

"What?" Gwennie was really good at this thing of changing subjects.

"You said you had a few questions to ask."

"Oh, yeah. Sex. I want to know a few things about it."

Gwennie spun around and stared at me in amazement. "You want to ask me about sex? I thought by now you knew all about the birds and the bees!" She laughed heartily.

"Course I do, nitwit. I just wondered ... well, you know, like sort of ..."

"Spit it out, Sam. Don't tell me Tony has been making suggestions?"

"Tony? Hell, no. I just wondered if maybe you and Richard ... well, you know ..."

Gwennie concentrated on her nails, and shifted about in her chair. She was plainly uncomfortable and I was about to tell her to forget it, when she said, "Yes, Sam. We did. I have nothing to hide. He is my fiancé and we will be married probably in April. Does that answer your question?"

Intrusive fool I am, yet I had to know more. "Yes and no. I just want to know if it is all that it is cracked up to be?"

Gwennie left off doing her fingernails. She put on that haughty look that she sometimes did. "Now you are definitely being inquisitive and quite out of place and I am not answering that question. Anything else on your cute little mind?"

I apologised. "One more thing. Who will be Richard's best man?"

"I would think Tony. Who else? Richard has no friends in Barbados."

I nodded. "Of course. Tony." Everything was leading back to Tony.

Well, not quite everything. Later on that day, I hopped on a bus and took a ride down to Holetown. I had finished my work in Wilfred's office and was at a loose end.

Holetown is a quaint little west coast town, teeming with history. It is where the first British settlers landed in Barbados and a monument is erected there to commemorate their landing.

The date of the actual discovery of Barbados is uncertain but there are records which give rise to the belief that in 1536 the Portuguese visited the island and named it *Los Barbadus* after the beautiful bearded fig trees which at that time grew in profusion throughout the island.

The Portuguese left and the island remained undisturbed until 1605, when a ship, the *Olive Blossom*, fitted out by Sir Oliph Leigh, put in at Barbados on her way to Guiana.

It would appear that after the visit of the *Olive Blossom,* the island slumbered undisturbed for another twenty-one years until Sir William Courteen, a wealthy London merchant, decided to equip an expedition.

His ship, the *William and John,* reached the island in 1626 with about forty Englishmen, who landed near the original landing place and founded Jamestown or what is now known as Holetown.

'Town', in my opinion, is a misnomer when describing Holetown. Village would be more fitting. A few houses, a police station with a courthouse attached, a dairy, funeral establishment and small grocery combined, and a small Methodist church which calls its followers to worship on Sunday mornings with its badly cracked bell. Holetown is full of character.

I jumped off the bus and went into the grocery store to buy some extra strong peppermints and just as I turned around to make my way back out, I ran smack bang into the brown-skinned boy from Boston Bay!

I said, "I'm sorry." He said, "I am not."

The very respectable coloured lady who had served me shook her head from side to side and said, "Albert Wetherby, you had better watch your step."

I turned and looked at her. "Oh, but it was my fault. I wasn't looking where I was going."

"Not if I know Albert, it was not." She gave him a knowing look and I thought she was being quite unfair. But I let it ride.

So – my brown-skinned boy's name was Albert. He was dressed in khaki shorts and a pale blue button-up shirt which was open to his midriff, showing the hairs on his chest. A floppy cloth hat adorned his head at a cocky angle.

He motioned to me to step outside the shop and we walked to where his bicycle was leaning against the wall. I opened the bag with the extra strong peppermints and offered him one. He, in turn, took out a packet of Wrigley's spearmint and offered me one. We both laughed and I settled for the gum while he took a peppermint.

"How did you get to Holetown?" he asked.

"Bus. I only came for some peppermints."

"You can get those at the little shop on the corner of my road. Much nearer."

"Thanks. I'll remember that."

"Would you like a lift back home? I have to pick up some milk from the dairy for my mum."

"A lift? In what?"

"*On* what. My bike, of course. I can bar you."

A lot of scary thoughts went whizzing through my brain with lightning speed. Imagine Wilfred seeing me on the bar of a coloured boy's bicycle! Better I settle for the electric chair. Or some malicious white Bajan spying me and jumping on the phone to Ellen or Wilfred with these shocking words: "I thought you ought to know that I just saw your daughter, Samantha, on a bicycle bar with a coloured boy." As my darling old Meg would have said, "Miss Sam, it going to be cat piss and pepper and licks fo' days when you gets home."

Albert interrupted my thoughts. "I know exactly what you're thinking, you know." I guess I blushed crimson. He continued, "Dr Wilfred would cut your tail if he found out. Right? No, don't start to shake your head. I know and you know that that's the truth. So perhaps you'd better bus it back home."

What a right balls-up. If I refused his offer, he might never speak to me again. Somehow that would be catastrophic. I wanted to continue our new-found friendship. I *liked* him. A whole heap. In fact, when he looked at me with his sexy eyes, I tingled all over. I had never had feelings like that before – not even with Tony.

I don't know where it came from – probably a wicked dead relative – but inspiration hit me and an inner voice said, '*Sam, take the bull by the horns and be damned the consequences.*'

Albert was bending over his bicycle reaching for the tire pump. I poked him in the back. "Hey. Go get the milk. I'm going to take that ride with you." That young man did not wait to hear those words twice. He shot into the store and was back out, carrying a pail of milk, before I had time to think of a guillotine. It would be stretching the truth a whole lot to say that I felt no apprehension during that ride back to Ginger Lily on Albert's bicycle bar. Yet it was an exhilarating-mixed-with-fear feeling that accompanied me on that dare-devil ride. Albert had lent me his hat to use as some form of disguise – I daresay to compensate me for my 'bravery' – and when we reached the row of casuarina trees alongside the road, just beyond the hedge surrounding Ginger Lily, he stopped the bike and I hopped off without incident. Little did I know that, not five minutes before, Wilfred had turned out of our driveway in his Austin car. Too close for comfort.

5

G WENNIE rushed into my bedroom, waving a letter in her hand.
"Guess what!" she yelled. I was lolling off in bed trying to
read a book to keep my mind off you know who from Boston Bay.
Gwennie did not give me time to guess what. She planted herself
down on the end of my bed and said, "Richard has been given
leave to get married, and they've shifted him onto the Harrison
Line *Spectator*, due in Barbados in two weeks time – that would be
March 15th!"

"Wow! That doesn't give us much time to make wedding plans."

"Oh yes, it does. Mum and I have been making plans from way
back when, and we only need to insert the date into the wedding
invitations and get them out. I have talked to most of the invitees
on the phone and warned them that they may have short notice,
so everyone will be ready."

I wriggled down to the bottom of the bed and put my arms
around her and popped a kiss on her cheek. "Gwennie, I'm so glad
for you, really I am. You are lucky to have a guy like Richard. He
really loves you. I mean, he could have buggered off after we
reached Barbados and never been heard of again. I just know you
will be happy. Just one favour – please don't let your sons follow in
their father's footsteps and go to school at Christ's Hospital, the
Blue Coat Boys. I can't take the thought of my nephews wearing
those ghastly long gowns!"

Gwennie returned my hug and roared with laughter. She
skipped out of the room as fast as she had skipped in. I heard her
yelling for Ellen, and then I returned to my book.

Not for long. I went into reverse gear and began thinking of our
childhood, and how very different we were. She the quiet, me-
ticulous one, the reader, the lover of material things – dolls in frilly
clothes, indoor games and books. I, the wild one, the tomboy,
swimming around and performing antics in the water and on the
beach, climbing trees and talking to them – the lover of nature.

Notwithstanding our differences, we were always there for each
other, especially when we had been at boarding-school. She was in

a form above me but we shared many school activities and outings together, mostly when it came to swimming and horse-riding. It was just lacrosse she couldn't stand.

And now here we were, I at a loose end, not knowing what to do with my life, and she getting married and probably going back to England to live, because that's where Richard's home was. I would miss her.

The phone rang, and Gwennie called me. "It's for you. Tony."

I went downstairs and picked up the phone. "Hi, Tony."

"*Que pasa*, kid?"

"*Nada*. What's up with you?"

"Just cool. Listen, Sam, I'm sorry about the other night when we couldn't go dancing after the movie but as you know, I was coming down with 'flu."

"Yes, I forgot. How are you feeling now?"

"I'm fine. Was wondering if we could go out this Saturday night?"

Oh, Tony, Tony. How I wish! It was not that I did not wish to go out with Tony, because he was such a nice guy, so thoughtful and considerate, and such a gentleman, but I could not help the nagging feelings gnawing away at my guts, preventing me from enjoying Tony's company in the way I should. When I was with him, sometimes I was miles away. Down Boston Bay – where else?

I sighed. "Okay, Tony. Saturday night it is." It was a lacklustre response, to say the least.

"You don't sound very enthusiastic, Sam." No fool, this Tony. Never was.

I tried to sound brighter. "Sorry, Tony. I had been lying down reading a book and I guess I was a bit drowsy. I really would love to go out Saturday night."

"Okay. Pick you up at eight o'clock. Till then, keep sweet."

We said our goodbyes.

The movie was a Mickey Rooney. Not my favourite actor by any means but the only cinema other than the grand Empire, where all the whites went on Saturday nights, was the Olympic. The flea-pit, they called it. It was cheaper, and no whites ever graced its doors.

Tony held my hand during the movie and he kept shifting about in his chair. I don't know what I was supposed to feel except perhaps a pleasurable inner glow, knowing that I was 'wanted', and yes, a little romantic – what with the darkness of the cinema and all.

After the movie, we drove to Club Morgan. Beautiful setting in spacious grounds on a hill overlooking the south coast with all its twinkling lights. It was *the* night spot – at least for the whites. No blacks were allowed in Club Morgan, except for the band members and Club Morgan staff.

A rhumba was playing. I love Latin American music. Tony found a waiter and got a table organised and we went to dance. I guess I got a bit carried away hip-movement wise and Tony responded by holding me tighter. Perhaps I would have been safer with a calypso because you can do your own thing without any body contact.

Is that what I was scared of? Body contact? Sex? Or was I afraid of falling in love with Tony? What the heck was 'falling in love' anyhow? Was it the peculiar thoughts that kept shooting through my brain – not to mention the feelings shooting through my body – when I thought of Albert? Al. That's what I would call him.

When we got back to the table, Tony ordered two rum punches from the hovering waiter.

"So you're going to be Richard's best man at Gwennie's wedding," I said to him.

"Yes. Gwennie asked me on behalf of Richard. Is he a nice guy?"

"Very. Terrific sense of humour and has a mischievous grin. I think he really loves Gwennie. They fell in love on board the ship coming home."

The waiter appeared and set the drinks on the table. "So I understand. Well," Tony said, raising his glass, "here's to them both." We toasted Gwennie and Richard.

Club Morgan was beginning to fill up and the band was warming up with a lively calypso.

It seems to me that when white Bajans let themselves go while dancing a calypso, they really let their hair down. They wiggle their hips crudely, wave their hands in the air and shout the words of the calypso – however vulgar they may be. At other times, when at work or in the course of their daily routines, butter wouldn't melt in their mouths and they are the epitome of respectability.

Of course, it is true to say that Club Morgan rum punches packed a powerful punch and went a long way to relieving the

Bajan whites of their inhibitions, and indeed, by the time Tony and I had polished off our respective rum punches, we joined the rowdy crowd on the dance floor and let our hair down. The drummer was thrilled at this exhibition and he drummed all the more provocatively, if it could be so described. Everyone was having a ball and the music seemed to get louder.

Tony and I were completely exhausted when we got back to our table, and we had to wait a while to order a drink as the nightclub was full and the waiters were all busy serving the half-drunk patrons.

Tony, now highly inebriated, grabbed my hand and said, "Let's go for a walk outside. It's warm in here." He took off his jacket and hooked it over the back of the chair.

The band had taken a break and outside, a soft breeze rustled through the mahogany and flamboyant trees, and the moon, though not full, shone through gaps in the trees and formed dappled patterns on the grass. Crickets and tree frogs were chirping their serenades to each other. Tony kept holding my hand.

"Sam, you know I will soon be going to Canada for two years."

I looked at him. He was so devilishly handsome! "Yes. I shall miss you when you go."

He seemed surprised. "Honestly?"

"Of course, Tony. Why are you surprised?"

"Well, sometimes you seem a little distant. You have a far-away look in your eyes. Did you leave a boyfriend in England?"

I laughed. Fat chance of that when I was stuck in a boarding-school where it was almost sacrilegious to speak of boys, let alone boyfriends. It was quite in order to have a crush on a girl, especially a prefect, or the headgirl. But I was never one to subscribe to those emotions. In fact, I had been horrified to discover that they existed.

"No, Tony. No boyfriend in England. Wilfred being what Wilfred is, would not have approved of my having a boyfriend at that age. He only lets me go out with you because he has known your family for such a long time, and you definitely have Wilfred's stamp of approval!"

"Well, what I'm leading up to is, could I be bold enough to ask you to wait for me while I'm in Canada?"

Incredible. "You mean become engaged?"

"Not exactly. Perhaps I am demanding too much. I mean, I wouldn't mind if you went to movies and dancing with other guys, but I would be very hurt if you became serious about someone."

Oh, woe is me, I thought. It's duck's guts for me. And the ducks are all running around the feet of the milch cow in the pasture at the home of Mr and Mrs Wetherby of Boston Bay.

"See what I mean? There's that far-away look in your eyes." Tony's voice chased the ducks with a full toss down the wicket. And then he leaned forward and kissed me ever so slowly and softly on the lips. Whoo! My emotions got all mixed up and confused and I felt more than a little light-headed. Blame the rum punch, I thought.

"Could I think about it, Tony? I can't answer that tonight."

He squeezed my hand and said, "Okay, but don't take too long." A shiver seemed to run through him, and I said, "Are you cold?"

"No, but I think we should go back in before I get carried away!"

When we got back to the table, we found Greta Laine and her escort seated there, waiting for us. Greta, a blonde, blue-eyed beauty, and her family, had also been residents of Strathmore when we had lived there but I had never particularly liked her. She always seemed so much more grown-up than the rest of us, and there was an air about her which seemed to proclaim, 'I am more knowledgeable and worldly than any of you.'

Quite frankly, I think I was a little afraid of her – afraid of saying something that she would consider dumb, and so I usually kept my distance.

Hellos were said all round, and Tony kissed Greta lightly on the cheek. She introduced her escort as Buddy. He was a tall, lanky young man, not particularly good-looking. Pimply face and bat ears.

"Sorry to invade your table but Greta wanted to say hello. We'll rejoin our party at a table over the other end of the room," said the well-mannered Buddy.

"Have a drink with us first," said Tony. Buddy appeared anxious to leave but Greta beamed at Tony. "Thanks, I'll have a rum and ginger, and Buddy will have a rum and soda." Greta had taken charge. She hadn't changed. I was slightly annoyed. But more was to come. Before the drinks were ordered, Greta skipped off to the dance floor, with Tony in tow. As I watched them, their bodies seemed to merge as one, although I have to admit that Tony looked plainly uncomfortable and he kept glancing back at me. Was I jealous? Yes, oddly enough I was.

The Buddy character and I barely exchanged a few pleasantries before Tony and Greta returned to the table. He too seemed a bit perturbed at the way Greta was behaving, and the evening was a little soured.

Greta decided to speak to me. Lucky me. "Well, Samantha, you're back from boarding-school in England. I hope you're not a lesbian ...," here she glanced at Tony with one of her knowing looks, "... but I don't imagine that with Tony in tow ..."

"*Greta*! That's uncalled for," interjected Tony, looking at me apologetically.

I, however, was not prepared to let it ride. I was suddenly no longer afraid of Greta, no longer in awe of her. I took up my glass and swallowed some rum punch. "No, I'm not a lesbian, but neither am I a hooking hussy."

Greta glared hatefully at me, and obviously swords were drawn. Buddy saved the day by hauling her off to dance, and before Tony could say anything to me, I hauled him off to dance.

When the dance finished, I excused myself and went to the ladies room and stayed there a long time on purpose. When I got back to the table, Greta and Buddy had mercifully left.

Tony pulled his chair close to mine and held my hand. "So, Miss Samantha Kinley, what do you intend to do with your life?"

I squirmed. I always squirm when people ask me that question because I honestly can't answer it. Look for a husband, have children and be a housewife? *Please!* Half of me is still living in the confined cocoon of a boarding-school with just girls and female teachers for company. I suppose I could defy the old man and go back to England and join the WRENS. Wouldn't be that much different from boarding-school! Regimentation, discipline, "*Yes ma'am; no ma'am; thank you, ma'am,*" salute. But that would probably mean not seeing Albert again. Not such a good idea.

Tony squeezed my hand. "You're off day-dreaming again, Sam."

I shook my head and looked at him. "Tony, if you want to know the truth, I haven't a clue what I'm going to do. I sure as hell don't intend to spend my life testing other people's pee and blood."

"You did 'O' and 'A' levels?"

"I did the old-fashioned Cambridge School Certificate and got a few credits which I believe are equivalent to 'O's. But, there's light at the end of the tunnel. Roy has offered me a job in his antique shop."

Tony suppressed a laugh. "And?"

"I'm going to take it. Fiddling about with antiques surpasses mucking about with pee any day, Tony."

Tony laughed heartily and gave me a hug. "That's my girl. Straight to the point."

The band started to play the lively calypso 'Mary Ann' which, after so many years, was still very popular and everyone jumped up to dance – or should I say jumped up to jump up. I don't know what made me look into Tony's eyes because it is not easy to fix your gaze on anything while you're shaking up your body, but I suddenly discovered something compelling in his eyes which sent a tingle through my body, and I couldn't figure out why. I mean, I had looked into Tony's eyes countless times when we were younger and hadn't found anything startling.

It was when I was in bed later that night, half asleep, that I bounced up and thought, 'Jeez, Tony's eyes are like Albert's!' I went back to sleep and dreamt of some character that was half Tony and half Albert.

6

How time flies! Here we were, past the halfway mark into 1951, and so many events seemed to have taken place during the first half.

In March, I started working with Our Boy Roy in his antique shop, after a ding-dong row with Wilfred. When I told him I had decided to go and work with Roy, he hit the roof. "*What?* You wish to go and work with that pansy boy?" he yelled. "You were doing fine with me. I am getting ready to negotiate with a laboratory in London to have you go there and train."

"As what – a lab technician?"

"For a start, but you could go further. Much further."

Yeah, I'll bet, I thought. Like mucking about with intracellular gonococci and other such charming bacteria and always having to watch out I don't spill horrible acids on my hands.

We had ranted and raved at each other for a while but I made it clear that I did not wish to become a lab technician and that was that. Wilfred and I did not speak to each other for about a week and I went merrily on my way into the antique world.

Then there was the grand event of Gwennie and Richard's wedding in April. That was some bash! Wedding service at Bridgetown Cathedral yet. Close on two hundred people crawling all over Ginger Lily, bumping into each other, drinks in hands and half-drunk grins on faces.

The driveway had been lit up like it was Christmas, and light and music poured from the house, as if in competition with the Marine Hotel – or so it seemed to me. The music was provided by a well-known lady pianist who played at all the so-called top class weddings and parties. Wilfred said he could not afford Percy Green's band. The lady pianist was good, and when she hit a calypso, everyone went hog-wild.

Richard looked dazzling in his all-white Merchant Marine officer's uniform, and Gwennie looked almost majestic in her wedding gown. I had never seen her look so happy and radiant.

Tony – well, I almost fell in love with Tony that evening, he looked so breathtakingly handsome. And when we danced, I felt close to heaven. I almost forgot Albert. Almost.

I drank too much champagne and when the wedding ceremony came to an end, after Richard and Gwennie had taken off, with the clanking tins tied to the back bumper of the taxi, for their honeymoon at the Crane Hotel, perched on a cliff on the south-east coast of the island, Wilfred and Ellen refused to let me go to Club Morgan with Tony. "It's bed for her, Tony, she's had far too much to drink," declared Wilfred, and when I rocked and swayed into bed, I mercifully passed out cold.

Tony left Barbados for two years of university in Canada. I didn't truthfully know how I felt about that. I was all mixed up. I did care for Tony and I missed him for sure, but my heart did not do all the funny things it did when I saw Al – not to mention peculiar stirrings throughout the rest of my body, which at times frightened me!

Roy was a pet. He was so understanding, I felt I could talk to him and confide in him about anything, and I knew he would not betray my confidence. I suppose in political terms you would call him a liberal. He was also free from racial prejudice and I think that is why we got along so well together. He knew that I was fully aware of his homosexuality and I think he never ceased to be amazed at my acceptance of this. "What a breath of fresh air!" he exclaimed when I expressed my opinion on such matters.

He fussed all over the shop, waving his hands about, moving the various *objets d'art* into different positions almost daily, talking to them all the while. "Now you, my little darling, you sit over here on this Napoleon table from Martinique – just so."

Roy's partner, Guy, from Martinique, a tall young man with closely cropped brown hair and very 'French'-looking, was quite charming. He was a little in awe of me at first. I daresay he expected me to be a prude. He probably also wondered if I had designs on his boyfriend, Roy.

Roy soon straightened him out, and the three of us got along like a house on fire.

My job with Roy was that of glorified housekeeper, for want of a better word. Roy insisted that I be called his 'assistant'. Basically, I helped deal with customers and more or less kept the furniture and objects polished and dust-free. There was a maid who did all the general dusting and sweeping but she was not allowed to touch the merchandise. Roy said that with most domestics, they just had to *look* at an object and it broke.

"Are you in love with Tony?" Roy shot the question at me one day out of the blue while he was fussing around with a Ming dynasty vase, and rocked me off my feet.

"Blimey, Roy, you do shoot straight from the hip!" I knew that Roy hated me to say 'blimey'. "It's very Cockney British," he would grumble.

Roy twittered. That's the best way I can describe his little laugh. "Well? Are you, or don't you want to answer that?"

I walked over to him to help him straighten a large painting that took up a good part of one wall. "I can't answer that question, Roy, because I don't honestly know."

He looked at me quizzically. "That's odd. You are either in love, or you're not. Take it from me."

"The expert?"

He did a little pirouette and cocked his head. "Exactly, *ma petite!*" He gave me a little chuck under the chin.

That day I confided in Roy. I tried to unravel my mixed-up thoughts and emotions because I knew he would be a sympathetic listener. I was even surprised at just how sympathetic he was.

"You do have a problem, my dear child, but it's not insurmountable."

"Roy, let me remind you that this *is* 'Victorian' Barbados."

"Ah yes, dou-dou, but even in Victorian Barbados, there are ways and means of doing things. Take me, for instance. I just do my own thing and to hell with what people think. I am a law-abiding citizen; I don't go out of my way to hurt people, I mind my own business, and if I offend society, that's their problem!"

"You have one advantage, Roy. You're a man."

Roy did not twitter. He put his hand up to his mouth and sniggered. "That's debatable, duckie!" I knew that Guy, who was busy at his desk doing some accounts, heard him, because he looked up and grinned.

A letter from Gwennie. In London. After a short honeymoon in New York.

Dear Sam,

How are you? Did Mum and Dad show you my letter? Since then, I have some terrific news – I am pregnant!

Richard has gone back to sea but he will be home again in six weeks, when he will be able to spend one week. I count the days until he is home again. However, we have made a big decision. We have applied to immigrate to Australia, where, under special provisions, we will be given a spot of land by the Aussie government, but we have to build our own house. We will travel out on one of the P & O liners at a very reasonable cost. This will all take place after I have the baby, which is due in February next year.

You know how I hate England, although so far it hasn't been dreadfully cold and the flat is well heated, but I hate housework! I could do with your darling Meg to help me.

I know if you were here you would be doing all kinds of things – rowing on the Serpentine nearby (we're in Bayswater), and perhaps you would even have a go at riding in Rotten Row! I wish I could be like you – always active.

On another topic – Wilfred would do his nut if he were here. London Transport, along with Lyons restaurants and some of the hospitals throughout Britain have made some sort of agreement with West Indian governments to employ West Indians and now we are seeing quite a few black faces in and around London. The British people seem to welcome them with open arms. I think it's the novelty but it will no doubt wear off when they see the standard of behaviour of these people and how prolific they are, then it will be'cat piss and pepper'!

I must close now and get some hateful housework done. Regards to everyone at home.

Love,
Gwennie.

Little did Gwennie know it, but Wilfred had already heard about the West Indian Workers To Britain scheme, and yes, he had done his nut when he heard it on the Rediffusion local news.

"Do you know what that man Adams has done?" he expostulated to Ellen, who was at the time dutifully watering her potted verandah plants. She glanced amusedly at him. "Tabled a resolution in the House to rid Barbados of white people?" she enquired, rather tongue-in-cheek.

Wilfred ignored her sarcasm. "Worse. We could always go and live in Canada, Australia or New Zealand. He has negotiated with the British Government to flood Britain with trash from Barbados."

Ellen made an appropriate face but kept her counsel.

"Do you know what that means?" Wilfred continued.

Ellen nodded. "I have a fairly good idea. It would ease the employment situation in Britain and at the same time ease the unemployment situation in Barbados," said Ellen, apparently undaunted.

"Ellen! Sometimes I think your brain was put in backwards."

Good old Ellen, sock it to him, I thought, as I took the watering can from her and said, "Let me help you water these plants before they get contaminated with Mr Adams' trash."

Wilfred was *furious*. He spun around and stamped out of the house and over to his office.

"You've upset your father," said Ellen.

"Mum, I'm sorry, but I do wish he would back off the racial issue. It seems to occupy his mind constantly and I'm sure it's not good for him."

"You're right, but he can't help it. We have to accept that, and perhaps just pretend to go along with it; humour him a bit. I've had to do that for years, remember?"

"You may be able to accept it, but I can't. It goes against my grain, and I can't be hypocritical."

"You're young and impetuous and you have a mind of your own, but for your father, life has not been exactly a bed of roses and he is resentful of a lot of things that happened when he was young. He can't change now."

"I understand – up to a point. But no one ever explains *why* life was not a bed of roses, nor of what he is resentful. A veil of secrecy is always drawn across any enquiries, and that tends to heighten my curiosity. Besides, what the hell does he have to complain about?" I swept my arm in an arc from the lawn to the beach. I wouldn't exactly call this seaside mansion a bed of thorns!"

Ellen looked exasperated. She plucked a dead leaf from an anthurium lily and cast it on to the pathway surrounding the lawn. Kellman would pick it up when he was doing his gardening. "Sam, do me a favour – please forget this conversation. I'm sorry, but you will just have to accept your father the way he is." End of story. Ellen turned on her heel and strolled inside the house, leaving me and my curiosity to our own devices.

There was a magnificent full moon. We had just had a dinner of split pea soup, roast leg of lamb, with baby potatoes sprinkled with parsley, fresh vegetables and side salad, followed by floating island dessert.

This was because we had company. A retired English army major and his wife who lived a mile or so north, along the coast. Funny pair they were – he smoked cigars and coughed his lungs up and she smelled of *4711 Eau de Cologne*, from a tiny bottle secreted in her handbag which she used to keep dabbing the cologne onto her face with a white lace hanky. She once ran out of *4711* and informed Ellen that she was forced to use *Soir de Paris* which she didn't care for because she hated frogs. It took me years to discover that by 'frogs', she meant French people.

The conversation at the dinner table had been mostly political, dominated by the major and Wilfred, and I couldn't wait to get away. They all retired to the veranda to have coffee and liqueur and I decided to stroll down the beach and sit under the old shak shak tree and gaze at the moon. I had to have a *tête-à-tête* with Kellman first, so I passed through the kitchen.

"Kellie," I said, patting him on the shoulder. "I am going down the beach and I don't wish you spying on me, regardless of what your orders are."

Kellman put on an innocent face and Meg, bless her, gave a knowing giggle and mumbled, "Lordy, looka trouble!"

I gave Meg a hug. "Fantastic English dinner, Meg, darling. You really outdid yourself. They'll soon have you doing roast beef and Yorkshire pud."

Kellman cleared his throat. "Excuse me, Miss Sam but you're in my way, and I am busy. I resent your comment about spying. I don't spy on people." He puffed himself up Jeeves-fashion and strode out of the kitchen.

The breeze wafting across from the sea was balmy as it gently teased the long shak shak pods, making them clatter. Some people call the shak shak 'woman's tongue' tree because of the clattering pods in a stiff breeze.

There were lights out on the horizon – a ship on her way out to far away places – and the masts of the fishing boats anchored in Boston Bay swayed from side to side. Lights from the houses along the bay cast a glow onto the white sand but the beach was quiet, except for the little ghost crabs scuttling about.

"Hi, Sugar Cake!"

I jumped. Cold shivers ran through my body like an electric current and it felt like things were growing out of my head, I was that scared.

"It's okay – it's me, Al."

I melted.

"Sorry I scared you. I thought you had seen me." He sat down on the sand beside me.

I automatically looked back towards the house to make sure Kellman wasn't lurking around, and then towards the veranda where Wilfred and Ellen and company were chatting. Albert followed my gaze. "Those your folks and friends on the veranda?"

"Yes. But it's not them I'm concerned about – it's Kellman." Albert knew Kellman because the last time we had spoken, just briefly, when I went to the shop at the corner of his avenue, he had told me how Kellman visits the rum shop regularly after work at night and drinks two beers. Never anything stronger, and never more than two beers.

"Kellman? He comes down the beach?"

"To spy on me."

Albert laughed heartily. "Oh boy, how you rich folks live! A butler spying on you!"

"Don't laugh, Al. He has been doing that since I was a child almost. He's like one of the family. As prejudiced as my father is, he believes the world begins and ends with Kellman."

"He pays him well, then."

I shrugged. "I guess," and as an afterthought, "By today's standards, that is." I stood up. "I think we should walk down the beach a little way, towards the sea grape trees where we can talk more freely and not be seen."

Albert jumped up. "I'm all for that."

We strolled down the beach slowly, looking back from time to time to make sure we weren't being followed. At times our bodies touched and I tingled and shivered all over. It was no use trying to deny these feelings now. They were crystal clear. I had a terrific crush on this guy and I was recklessly riding a rollercoaster – up or down, I knew not which way. Where it would all lead to, God only knew.

We sat by the sea grape trees and Albert held my hand. Then he kissed me, and I don't know where I went to, but I sailed through the air, up past the clouds and onto the moon, I'm sure. All caution was thrown to the wind. I did not even spare a thought for Tony.

I don't know how long the kiss lasted because I had lost track of time, but Albert eventually drew away and let out his breath. "Whew!" he exclaimed and shook his head. "Where did you learn to kiss like that?"

I was stunned. "*Me*? That was you doing all the kissing."

"Wanna bet?" But before I could answer, he grabbed my shoulders and pulled me towards him and kissed me again. I did not see the Wizard of Oz, but I know how Judy Garland felt when she took a trip Over The Rainbow.

I guess we were both pretty shaken up and I began to worry a bit, having lost track of time. "I think we should go," I said, standing up. He did not protest but gave me a hug and a little kiss before we strolled back up the beach, ghost crabs scuttling away in all directions under our feet while the tall casuarinas, bathed in brilliant moonlight, cast weird shadows along the beach, and the waves lapped gently on the shore. It was low tide and parts of the rocky reef could be seen sticking up out of the water.

No doubt about it, I was hopelessly in love, I thought, as we parted company – he towards Boston Bay and I up the pathway towards the house where the folks were talking and laughing on the veranda. No sign of Kellman. He was not required to stay late to serve drinks unless it was a party, so he must have gone off to the rum shop in Boston Bay to have his two beers.

I stayed awake for ages that night in bed, thinking of Albert and remembering every moment of the evening, reliving it over and over again. The soft yet demanding touch of his lips, and his hands occasionally brushing my breasts, not daringly, but gently and swiftly.

I was wrong about Kellman. On Sunday Ellen and Wilfred went off to church at St Michael's Cathedral. They tried to get me to tag along as there was a special service with a visit from an English Bishop. I declined. Since schooldays in England, I had become cheesed off with the Anglican church and opted to attend the services at the Congregational Church to which we had to walk in a 'croc' every Sunday. For one thing, the choirboys in the Congregational Church were far better-looking than the Anglican ones and a lot more daring too. If you stared at them long enough, they winked at you.

Kellman approached me out of the blue while I was writing my diary on the veranda. "Miss Sam, I would like to have a word with you."

"Sure, Kellie, be my guest. But aren't you supposed to be off duty today?"

"Yes, I am, but this is important."

I began to get scared. This was not typical Kellmanism. "What's on your mind? Sit down."

You could almost see the shock waves running through Kellman. He cleared his throat. "Now, Miss Sam, you know that would be out of place for me. I will remain standing and I will get straight to the point. You are heading for trouble – you and that young man, Albert Wetherby."

I sighed. "You've been spying again, Kellie."

"I already told you, Miss Sam, I do not spy on you. You are not a child, but I can't help seeing things if they happen to be within my sight, which is what you and Albert were on the beach last night."

My blood ran cold. How much had he seen, and if he wasn't spying, then how could he know? Before I could comment, he continued. "After I finished work last night, I went up the beach to Boston Bay and I saw you and Albert walking, hand in hand, coming from the direction of the grape trees. You could not see me because I was in the shadow of the manchineel trees."

I nodded my head. "So you *were* spying, if you were hiding under the manchineels. Furthermore, Kellie, it is none of your business, and as you said, I am not a child. What do you plan to do – tell my father?"

Kellman looked taken aback. "Of course not, Miss Sam, and you are right that it is none of my business, but you see, I happen to know Albert, and I know that he can only hurt you. He comes from a very respectable, hard-working family. His father and mother have a little farm, and his brother owns a fishing boat. They are decent people, but ..."

"Not my class. Go on, say it."

"Exactly so."

I looked at him and smiled. "Kellie, Ah do declyah," I said, trying to imitate a good ole' Dixie accent, "You sho' do remind me of ole Uncle Remus. Is you gonna go whump that l'il ole piccaninny Albert?"

Kellman drew himself up to his full height. He was not a short man. "You're making sport of me, Miss Sam, and if that is your attitude then I will say no more. If you think I am out of place, I'm sorry for that, but I felt it my duty to warn you, and maybe some day you will thank me." He marched off, leaving me sitting there feeling like a fool. I had hurt his pride. I guess I should have run behind him and apologised, but I was too stubborn.

I could not help wondering what he meant when he said that Albert could only hurt me. Because of his 'class' or his colour? Or both? I shook my head. Perhaps it was just 'Kellmanism'.

I wrote in my diary, '*Good old Jeeves has found out about me and Albert. I must confide in Roy.*'

7

Roy was skittering all over the shop like a little bird searching for an appropriate place to deposit the piece of straw in its mouth with which to build a nest. In this case it was a pencil that he had in his mouth and he was making little marks on the wall where he wanted to hang pictures.

I had met Mr and Mrs Wetherby and I was just about to reveal all to Roy. He already knew that I had a crush on Albert. What he did not know was that I was head over heels in love.

"So, my princess, you think so highly of this Albert that you had to go and meet his parents?" Roy mumbled with the pencil stuck between his teeth.

"Something like that, yes. I walked over to their farm the other evening after work. I had seen Albert in Holetown and told him I would like to meet them. He was quite chuffed."

Roy's head bobbed up and down and he mumbled, "Go on."

"Mrs Wetherby is a short, busy little woman with a light brown skin, very warm and hospitable. She was in her kitchen fussing over a cake she had just baked. She cut a slice for me. It was delicious."

"And he?"

"Mr W? A fairly thick-set man, also light brown-skinned, almost East Indian in appearance, with slick greyish curly hair and pale eyes. His father was a Trinidadian. He was pleasant enough but there was a wary look in his eyes, as if he did not quite trust me. He did not stick around but excused himself and went out to tend his sheep."

"You can hardly blame him for seeming a bit distrustful, duckie. It isn't every day that a white Barbadian female goes visiting the coloured parents of her boyfriend!"

I laughed. "It isn't every day that a white Bajan female has a coloured boyfriend either."

"You can say that again." He had removed the pencil from his mouth. "Thing is, where is this all going to lead? I mean, obviously it's going to get more serious. Sam, don't do anything stupid like getting pregnant if it's just going to be a casual love affair."

The phone rang. I answered it. "For you, Roy."

He whispered, "Who is it?"

"The old git who came in the other day enquiring about a double-end sofa."

Roy took the phone and covered the mouthpiece. "Woman's a pest. I told her I was trying to get one for her. Oh, never mind, I'll talk to her."

I cleaned a brass kettle while Roy talked to Mrs What's-her-name. When he was finished he came over to me and said, "Now where were we? This is a serious issue and we have to work it out."

"You were saying I shouldn't get pregnant. Fat chance of that when we can only find time for quick stolen kisses."

"Just as well, I'd say. At least until we see what develops. This Albert – is he well educated, and what does he plan to do with his life in terms of work?"

"Roy! You sound like a parent."

"Well, duckie, that's what I'll have to be – on a temporary basis at least – because you sure as hell can't go to them!"

"Every Barbadian is well educated, Roy, you know that. Albert went to Combermere School, but dropped out in fourth form because his father was ill and he had to go help his mother on the farm. He was sixteen. Naturally he did not do School Certificate. He is not qualified to do anything so he will just continue helping his parents on the farm and eventually take over when his old man passes away."

Roy nodded. "I see."

There was little left to say at that stage, but I felt as if a great weight had been lifted from my shoulders. Roy was not in the least scornful of my actions and, in fact, I think he honestly wanted to help me find a solution to the problem. The problem being that if Albert and I became serious about each other, what then? Would I have to marry him secretly and go and live on the farm with the Wetherby's? And face Wilfred's wrath? Not to mention scorn from friends and family! Would I be courageous enough to do that?

Fate intervened. As fate is sometimes wont to do. Aunt Lucy died. Aunt Lucy was not a real aunt but just a very close friend of Ellen's, who lived at a huge old plantation house way up in St Thomas, which is in the middle of Barbados. She was a spinster who lived all alone except for an elderly cook who had living quarters in the basement of the house. She also had a chauffeur. He did not live in.

Aunt Lucy had always been very fond of me for some obscure reason, and after an illness, when I was about ten years old, Ellen and Wilfred had sent me to stay with her to convalesce. I was not to have any excitement, said the doctor.

The doctor did not get his way. Excitement was definitely on the agenda at Cumberland House. Aunt Lucy spoilt me rotten. She bought all kinds of toys, games and books for me and we were chauffeur-driven all over the island in her huge American Dodge. She also took me on a visit to St Lucia, a neighbouring island, where we stayed with her friends in a large house up the Morne, overlooking Castries.

She took me into Bridgetown and outfitted me with lots of shirts and shorts (she knew I hated dresses) and then we had lunch at the Tip Top Tea Shop, close to Lord Nelson's statue (which was erected, believe it or not, before the one in Trafalgar Square, London).

I had been to visit her just once since returning from school in England. She was now very old and semi-invalid but she had retained her sense of humour, and when I kissed her, she said, "Gracious, I see you're wearing a dress! I hope school in England hasn't turned you into a prudish little snob!"

And now she was dead. Ellen was sobbing in her bedroom. I went to comfort her. "She was very fond of you, Sam," she sobbed.

"I know. I was fond of her too. She was so young at heart."

"The lawyer telephoned today and said he would like to see you and me in his office."

"*Me?*"

"Yes. Both of us. She has probably left a little jewellery or something for us."

I was surprised and I couldn't wait to find out what she had left me. Probably her little mahogany antique writing bureau which I had always admired.

I was not prepared for the shock I got. Along with the said writing bureau, Aunt Lucy had left me ten thousand Barbados dollars, plus five hundred pounds in a bank in London. She had left Cumberland House to Ellen and hundreds of dollars to the RSPCA. She was a devoted animal lover.

I walked out of the lawyer's office in a dream. My head was spinning. *Ten thousand dollars!* No doubt Wilfred would advise me exactly how to spend it.

When we got home, I ran into the kitchen and hugged Meg. "You know the kerosene stove you said you saw at the hardware store and said you would like for your little house? Well, you're going to get it."

Meg was accustomed to my sudden outbursts of passion towards her but she was quite unprepared for this. "What you talking about, Miss Sam?"

"I said, you can dump your old wood and coal stove. I'm going to buy you the oil stove." I skipped out of the kitchen leaving her with her mouth open.

Aunt Lucy's funeral at St Thomas Parish Church was a quiet, sombre affair. She had few relatives in Barbados. Many of them had buzzed off years ago, some to England, and some to the USA.

All of her friends in Barbados attended the funeral, along with her old cook and the chauffeur and a surprising number of black people from the surrounding area. It was said that she had been kind to many people, helping them financially from time to time with their house repairs, and they had come to pay their respects.

In due course, my ten thousand dollars was deposited in a bank account and I began to entertain some very interesting thoughts as to how I would spend it. Just as I thought, Wilfred made suggestions on how I should invest it but I ignored these. I was planning to return to England, but not alone. I would take Albert with me – if he wanted to go. At least he could learn a trade at a polytechnic. All sorts of thoughts began to whirl around in my excited brain and I couldn't wait to talk to Albert.

I got the opportunity when Ellen said she had run out of thread for the sewing machine and she would have to make a trip into Bridgetown, which she hated doing because it was so hot and sticky.

"I can go to Holetown and get it for you," I offered.

"Aren't you going to work?"

"Yes, but if you can wait until tomorrow, I can get it from the little store in Holetown. The lady sells just about everything in there, including haberdashery stuff, and she opens on Saturdays."

"Well, if you don't mind."

"No, I don't. I love going to Holetown."

Saturday morning, bright and early, I darted off up the road to the Wetherby farm. I found Albert milking a cow. He was very surprised to see me. "What brings you here so early?" He could not get up, so I sat on a stool beside him.

"I have some exciting news. When you've finished milking, could you go to Holetown with me – by bus?"

"Something exciting happening in Holetown?"

"No, silly. I have to talk to you, but I have to go to Holetown to get something for my mother."

"Give me ten minutes. I've almost finished here and then I have to take these two pails of milk in to the old lady."

"You got all that milk from one cow?"

Albert roared with laughter. "We have more than one cow, you know."

"So where are the others?" I looked around under the shed, which was divided into stalls, all of which were covered with dry grass. I thought to myself, not a bad life, farming. I wouldn't mind trying my hand at it. But not right away. I had other plans.

"They're out on the pasture," said Albert.

Albert finished his chores, washed his face and hands, put on clean clothes, and we walked to the bus stop together, ignoring the inquisitive faces peeping from behind curtains in the few houses along the avenue.

The bus was practically empty, with just three or four people – one of whom, unfortunately, happened to be Cyrus, the policeman. Cyrus was a top class cop but a notorious nosy parker, and he and Wilfred were great friends – if the word 'friend' is applicable to Wilfred's relationship with a black person. Just as Wilfred thought the world of Kellman, so too did he believe that Cyrus was the greatest policeman in the island – if not the world.

I noticed with some consternation the look on Cyrus's face when he realised that Albert and I were together. The bus started to move off.

"Wait, Jackman, don't move yet," Cyrus's voice piped up from two seats away. The other passengers, along with Albert and I, looked at Cyrus.

Cyrus addressed Albert. "Young man, who you think you is?"

Albert did not appear intimidated by Cyrus. "I am Albert Wetherby. What do you want with me?"

"I know who you is, you idiot. I wants to know who you *think* you is. You can't sit next to her."

Albert looked at me and then at Cyrus. "You have a problem with the young lady?"

Cyrus was furious. "You knows damn well who my problem is with. I tell you, you can't sit with her. She is white."

"So this is South Africa?" Albert asked Cyrus. I was thoroughly enjoying the fracas, but not without some reservations. I knew that Cyrus was not only capable of calling Wilfred on the phone to tell him, but very likely to.

"Excuse me, Cyrus," I pitched in, "My mother asked Albert to go with me to Holetown to pick up something for her." Hell, white lies don't hurt.

Cyrus thought for a moment. The other passengers were leaning forward, anxious to see how this would end. It was not often that such excitement occurred on a bus and they were loving it.

Jackman, the driver, glanced back. "I could drive now?" he enquired politely.

"You will drive when I tells you to drive," replied Cyrus.

Cyrus was not satisfied. "It appear to me that if Mrs Kinley want something from Holetown that are too heavy for you, she would send Kellman."

"I never said it was too heavy. Anyway, what has it got to do with you, Cyrus?"

Cyrus had never been spoken to like that and he was not pleased. I knew for sure that he would report me to Wilfred. Suddenly I didn't care. I threw caution to the wind. "Albert is right, Cyrus, this is *not* South Africa, nor is it Alabama, Georgia or Louisiana, and I would thank you to mind your own business."

Cyrus was thoroughly squashed. He was embarrassed, and what made it worse was that the other passengers giggled.

Cyrus unleashed his wrath on them. "Don't be laughing at me, you hear? Don't forget I is Cyrus," he huffed. "Drive, Jackman," he ordered.

The journey to Holetown continued peacefully.

Albert waited for me on the beach, where I joined him after purchasing the thread from the store. He was perched on the bows of a little dinghy on the sand.

"We can't stop long, Al, because my mother is waiting for the thread. The exciting news is that an old lady friend of my mother's died and left me some money. I would like to return to England, but ..." I hesitated, and looked him full in the eyes, "not without you."

Albert's eyes opened wide as he stared at me in disbelief. "Wait. Am I hearing you right? You wish me to go to England with you?"

"That's what I said."

"Even after that little incident on the bus, knowing the social situation in Barbados?"

I nodded slowly. "Particularly after that. Cyrus's attitude puts that situation right into a nutshell. Al, you said you love me. I love you. We can't go to movies or dancing together; we're even taking a risk being seen together. It should not be so, and I firmly believe that one day things will change, in the not too distant future, but if we went to England for a while, you could do a trade or something, if you cared to, and we could go out together. It's a very different atmosphere and society."

Albert was gazing down at the sand and shuffling his feet about. He kicked sand at a little ghost crab peeping out of its hole. "You see him? He is totally free. He can come and go on this beach as he pleases, he can mingle with the other crabs – even the technicolour ones – and the only things they fight about are food and sex. But us? You and me? Girl, we have to fight society because I have a brown skin and you have a white skin. You really think it would be any different in England?"

"You forget I lived in England, Al. London is very cosmopolitan and people tend to mind their own business. You live next door to people for years and never get to meet them. Many different races mingle together in London. Maybe in small villages you would find the same prejudices but not in London and the larger cities. I just think that if we wish to be together, we would have to leave Barbados, for the time being, at least."

Albert shrugged and looked doubtful. Had I been tuned in, I would have picked up the right vibes. But I was blind with love for this bloke and I just wanted to be with him forever. He, in turn, had said as much to me, and I believed him.

"Give me a little time to think it over, Sugar Cake. It sounds good but see, I never gave much thought to what lies beyond the farm and my folks, and it never occurred to me to do anything but to follow in my father's footsteps. Just let me think it over, okay? I mean, I know you could not marry me or live on the farm with me because you would be cut off from all your friends and family and eventually it would get to you. Am I right?"

I nodded slowly. He was right. It would cause conflict between him and me, his family and me and him and his family. It could only end disastrously.

We agreed to think it over and talk about it some more, and we left the beach and walked to the bus stop. We sat very close together on the bus which I believe caused some of the passengers a certain amount of discomfort. Or so it seemed.

8

A summons to Wilfred's office made itself known via Ellen at breakfast one morning soon after my *tête-à-tête* with Al. I had noticed that whilst eating her soft-boiled egg perched in a hen-designed egg cup, she appeared to be hesitant and slightly uncomfortable. She fiddled with the spoon, glanced at me and fiddled some more.

"Dad wishes to see you in his office immediately after breakfast," she announced.

"What about?"

"It is not for me to tell you. You must wait and hear what he has to say."

I made my way over to Wilfred's office after bolting down a quantity of cereal – the type that bloats you out and makes you want to 'go' – in the hopes that it would act fast and I would have an excuse to get out of his office.

I knocked on the door and entered his office. "Mum said you wanted to see me," I said, all wide-eyed with innocence although I was pretty sure I knew what it was about. Either Cyrus or Kellman had been talking.

He pointed to the extra chair. "Sit down." I sat. He cleared his throat, took off his glasses and polished them on a tissue. "Samantha, why are you so different from everyone else in the family? Why are you so cantankerous?"

"Me? Cantankerous?"

"Yes. You are full of ideas bordering on, I hate to say, *dangerous*. You are forever fraternising with low-class black people and you are lowering yourself to their level."

Oh boy. Now I'd heard it all. Was this for real? *Lowering* myself? I stared at him and shook my head in disbelief. "Did you say *lowering* myself? Am I supposed to be God?"

Wilfred banged his fist on the desk. "Don't be rude, Samantha!" he yelled. "It has been reported to me that you have been seen regularly visiting the Wetherby place over by Boston Bay. Why do you go there? Those people are not your class nor colour."

I belched. From nervousness. "Colour? Did you say *colour?* Class is one thing, Dad. Colour is quite another. Which do you mean?"

Wilfred looked at me in amazement. He was clearly thrown for a loop. "See what I mean about your being cantankerous? You know perfectly well what I mean. The Wetherbys are coloured. They are also working-class people. Not your kind. You know perfectly well that there are some very decent middle-class black people but you choose the low-class ones. What can you learn from them and why do you visit them?"

"Learn from them? Well, farming for a start. Mr Wetherby is a farmer. He lives off the land. He grows corn and sweet potatoes and vegetables. He has fruit trees. He has cows and sheep so he doesn't have to buy milk or mutton. He feeds his family and others. He is self-sufficient. That, in my book, says a whole heap."

"Very enterprising of Mr Wetherby. I have a great deal of respect for the man. He is a humble, decent man but he is not educated and he knows his place."

He knows his place. "And what is 'his place', Dad? Does it entail bowing and scraping to you, taking his hat off, moving off the sidewalk onto the road and saying, 'Morning, mistress' when he sees Mum coming along? Does it mean that his offspring should be nothing but farmers or fisherfolk – likewise their offspring, *ad infinitum*? Is that what you mean by 'knowing his place'?"

Wilfred's eyes blazed. He looked totally exasperated. He kept shifting about in his chair and taking off his glasses and putting them back on. He shook his head from side to side. Then he stretched out his arms on his desk and laid his head between them. I almost felt sorry for him. But I had no intention of softening up and agreeing with him.

"Why are you giving me these problems?" he asked, sighing. "Gwennie never behaved like this. Why are you deliberately hurting your mother and me?" Head still resting on the arms.

"Dad, I am not deliberately hurting you and Mum. However, I would like you to understand that I am an *individual*. I have my own likes and dislikes. I have my own ideas and thoughts. I am not a puppet. I am me. I am not you, I am not Mum, I am not Gwennie. I am *me*. And I am not a child any more."

Wilfred sighed and lifted his head. He was subdued but not ready to give up the fight. He sucked his teeth. "I spent a considerable sum of money sending you and Gwennie to school in England in order to allow you to mix with girls of your own class and standards of upbringing, and what do you do? You come back here and go mixing up with Yahoos. I just do not understand why."

It was my turn to sigh. I wondered if this were the right time to tell him what I knew about his family background. I thought better of it. I might give the old geezer a heart attack and I'd never be able to live it down.

"Dad, I appreciate what you did for my education, but as a matter of fact, paradoxically, sending me to England had the opposite effect. It broadened my outlook on life. I met girls there who had no hang-ups about colour and they never talked about class. Perhaps that was because they *had* class, since that's what we're on about. They knew that the maid, cook, gardener or whomever their parents employed, were of a different class, yes, but it never occurred to them to talk about it, let alone keep on harping on about it."

"Would any of them have married the gardener's son?"

I smiled and shook my head slowly. You don't give up, old man, do you! "That would perhaps be unusual, but ..." I cleared my throat significantly, "... it has happened in the best of families."

Wilfred swiveled his chair around and glared at me furiously. "Well, by damn, it's not going to happen in *this* family while I am alive. Is that clearly understood?"

It was at this point that my bowels evicted their gaseous substance in a little 'pop' that was clearly heard in the silence of the office. "Excuse me, but I must go." I got up and left him leaning back in the chair with his hand on his forehead. As I left, I could imagine the hand slipping down to cover his nose.

Wilfred and I avoided each other as much as possible after that. We were polite to each other but that was as far as it went. Ellen was quite upset over it. She said she couldn't understand why we were always at loggerheads and wouldn't I please try not to upset my father.

I continued to see Al as often as I could and I visited the Wetherby farm from time to time. I was glad that I could escape from Ginger Lily every day to work in Roy's shop. I had travelled by bus at first but Roy insisted on picking me up on mornings and dropping me home on evenings, which meant going out of his way. But Roy was that sort of person.

One morning, while Roy and I were driving up the road towards Bridgetown, I spied Albert on his bicycle with a dishy-looking brown-skinned girl sitting on the bar. They were riding in the opposite direction, probably heading for Holetown. My heart did a flip and a hot flash of jealousy shivered through my body. I grabbed Roy's arm and nearly caused him to steer the car into the gutter. "There's Albert, Roy." I pointed towards the bicycle. Roy slowed down.

"Him – on the bicycle, with the girl on the bar?"

"Yes."

"Wow! Real good-looker. I could fancy him myself! But who's the girl on the bar?"

I did not answer immediately so he glanced at me. "Uh-oh. Trouble, huh?"

I shrugged. "I don't know, Roy. Could be a relative."

"But you're burning up with jealousy, anyhow."

"Yes." Albert had not even glanced in our direction yet he knew Roy's car.

"Roy, look out!" Roy swerved to avoid killing a dog that ran across the road, plunged down on to the beach just by an open 'window to the sea' at Paynes Bay and dashed into the sea for its morning swim. I couldn't blame it, for the water looked glorious in the sparkling morning sunlight, and the tree-shaded beach looked decidedly inviting.

"Sorry about that," said Roy. "I was about to ask you how serious this thing is between you and Albert. I mean, have you been … well, you know what, with him?"

I stared at him in horror. "Roy! How many times have I told you – NO! I can't take a chance like that. We have been seeing each other as often as possible, exchanging a few stolen kisses, but no sex. As it is, Wilfred is on my case and getting suspicious."

"Well, excuse me, sweetie, but you can't blame the guy if he messes around with someone else – someone who is prepared to go the whole way. He looks very sexy to me. How long do you plan to keep him waiting?"

"Roy, you're incredible, you know that? I told you, we have talked it all over, and he is thinking about going to England with me. He said he will let me know the answer shortly. When we get to England, we can do anything and *everything*. Does that satisfy you?"

Roy laughed. "It satisfies me, duckie. Question is, does it satisfy *him*?"

We spent the entire journey to Bridgetown discussing Albert and me, and Roy said he and Guy would miss me from the shop but if he could do anything to help with the situation, he would do it with pleasure. Roy loved a little intrigue.

As it turned out, he was of considerable help when the time came, for soon after that Albert and I met on the beach at Holetown and he told me he would go to England with me.

I had tackled him about the girl on the bicycle bar and he had laughed and said she was his cousin. I believed him.

"There is an Elders & Ffyfes banana boat with passenger accommodation leaving for Southampton in two weeks' time, or we can wait until next month's sailing. I can be ready in two weeks. Can you?" I asked him.

He answered immediately. "I sure can." I was taken aback by his apparent haste. It was so different from his first reaction. He noticed my hesitation. "What's wrong – don't you believe me?"

"I hope I can. I was so overwhelmed by your immediate reaction that I was caught off guard!" He gave me a peculiar look which I could not quite define.

He clapped his hands together. "So, what are we waiting for? Let's go home and get packed!" He grabbed me in a bear hug and we danced around on the sand.

The next day, Roy and I went to the office of the agent for Elders & Ffyfes and I booked my cabin on the *Golfito* while Roy booked one for Albert – just in case the agent was a nosy parker. There was only one class of accommodation. All outside cabins, en suite. Beautiful. I was not going to give Albert a chance to change his mind.

Roy pretended to cry when we got to the shop. He held his hands up to his face. "God, I hope you're doing the right thing, lovey."

"Course I am, Roy, and come off that crying act!" I went over to him and kissed him on the cheek. "But it's nice to know you care."

"Listen, if anything goes wrong, you let me know right away, you hear?"

I hugged him. "I will, I will. But nothing will go wrong." Famous last words.

I told Ellen and Wilfred that evening that I had booked my passage to England. Ellen's facial expression was a mixture of emotions. She seemed sort of relieved yet somehow a little sad. Wilfred was in his seventh heaven. He did not jump up and do a calypso but he came pretty close to it. Getting rid of the Trouble Tree at last! He came over to me and hugged me which surprised both Ellen and me.

"My child, you are doing the right thing. I prayed that you would. Of course you know that Mum and I will miss you, and you and I have had our differences, but I think a year or two in England will do you the world of good. You go with my blessings, and Mum's, of course." He glanced at Ellen and she nodded agreement. Of course.

The two weeks before departure date simply flew. Ellen spent most days at her sewing machine making blouses out of thick material for me, and in the evenings she knitted furiously away at a woollen cardigan. It was already autumn in England.

I had visited the Wetherby farm for the last time, to say goodbye to Mr and Mrs W. Mister was his usual 'distant' self, just shaking my hand and wishing me well. Mrs Wetherby hugged me and held me off to look into my eyes. "I hope you two young people know what you're doing. This is not an easy world, especially where mixed relationships and marriages are concerned. I am losing my Albert. You are gaining him. Look after him for me, okay?"

I assured her that I would and I squeezed her hand.

It was very difficult saying goodbye to Meg again and we both cried. She hugged me and whispered, "God bless and take care of you. I ain't happy 'bout what you doing but I hopes it work out for you."

I shook Kellman's hand and was more than a little surprised to see tears in his eyes. He shook his head in the negative and said, "I am going to pray for you." I knew then that both Kellman and Meg were suspicious of mine and Albert's plans. It is pretty nigh impossible to keep a secret in Barbados and I've no doubt that Kellman heard a rumour or two in the rum shop while slurping his two evening beers.

I was a little disturbed by their reference to God having to 'take care of me'. True to say that Bajan black people were fiercely religious but why was everyone so deeply concerned, especially as Albert and I would be away from this environment.

The Day had arrived and here we were – a group of about thirty, made up of family and friends – waiting, once again, at the Baggage Warehouse in Bridgetown to say our final goodbyes. Roy and Guy were here – Roy dressed in a bright pair of red slacks and a pastel pink shirt, and Guy in very French-looking short shorts and a sports shirt. There were kisses and handshakes, tears and smiles, and then Ellen, Wilfred and I stepped onto the tender which would convey us over to the *Golfito,* anchored in Carlisle Bay.

I glanced around and saw Albert entering another tender with some other people, having said goodbye to his parents on the quayside.

The ship was sailing at six p.m. I was full of very mixed emotions. How well I remembered not so long ago arriving at Carlisle Bay on board the *Lady Rodney,* and how excited I was. Now I was leaving Barbados, not knowing when or if I would ever be back, and it hurt like hell. I was being forced to leave for reasons which shouldn't exist. At the same time, I was entering a new phase of my life with the man I loved, and that alone was exciting.

After I had stashed my stuff in the cabin, Ellen, Wilfred and I sat in the saloon and had drinks. Ellen kept giving me affectionate looks and checking that I had everything and had done everything there was to do, and Wilfred gazed about admiringly at the saloon decor and smiled at me from time to time like the pussycat that swallowed the mouse. I thought, *if he only knew!*

The all-ashore gong banged and there were tearful goodbyes. Up came the anchors and the *Golfito* slipped silently out of Carlisle Bay. Goodbye, Barbados.

9

ENGLAND

The *Golfito* ploughed her way across the Atlantic without incident although the weather was not the best, the seas were often running high, and the ship pitched and rolled. Miraculously I was not seasick and neither was Albert. Many nights he sneaked into my cabin, and other nights I sneaked into his. Eventually I would get around to writing to Gwennie, who was then in Australia with Richard, to tell her that sex was fantastic, but not yet because she knew nothing of my 'elopement', and, if I revealed it, she might go into shock!

Initially, the Purser had placed Albert and me at separate tables but I soon rectified that and asked to have Albert sit at my table. If this caused a bit of a stir among the ship's officers and dining room stewards, I pretended not to notice. As to the passengers, they were a motley crowd. A few middle-class blacks and a few white Barbadians who did not even bother to hide their stares at Albert and me. But I had long since thrown caution to the wind.

The Bay of Biscay lived up to its fame. It was *rough*. We spent an entire day and night tossing and turning, pitching and rolling, and it was now too chilly to sit out on deck. The sun seemed to have disappeared forever.

Southampton at last. Boat train to Waterloo. What memories! November 1945, arriving at Southampton on board the New Zealand Line *Rangatiki*, which had been turned into a troop ship bringing back troops from the Far East, along with scores of children who had been evacuated to New Zealand and Australia for the duration of the war; sailing all the way up the English Channel on full alert. All passengers and crew had been ordered to wear life-jackets non-stop – sleep in them and all – for two days, because of the possibility of German mines in the Channel.

How different this time. I booked first class on the train for Albert and me because I was damned if I was going to share a compartment with a bunch of white Bajans who would spend the entire journey staring at us. We had a compartment to ourselves and we took the opportunity to kiss and hug and fondle. At last we were together and FREE!

Good old Waterloo – still much the same, but a lot cleaner. The little News Cinema way over in the corner, and W.H. Smith, and other booths in the centre of the station. Familiar territory. Now to find a taxi and an hotel.

We checked into a small hotel in Queensway . There was a partial view of Hyde Park from the bedroom window. It was raining – as usual. Hello, London.

"Is it always like this in England?" Albert was standing by the window looking out. "We've had nothing but grey skies since the Bay of Biscay. I hate it." He turned around to face me.

I went over and put my arms around him. "I told you – the weather is not England's most redeeming feature, to say the least, but honey, we have to be practical. If we wish to be together, we have to put up with a lot of inconveniences. It won't be forever, you know that." I kissed him.

"You got that right. At least it won't be forever for me."

This rather disconcerting remark registered in my brain but then I had to remember that Albert had given up the freedom of a farm life in glorious all-day sunshine to be cooped up in a small hotel room in cold, rainy London. He must have felt like a caged animal.

"Tomorrow we're going to start house-hunting, but right now, let's get unpacked. We'll have to stay in this hotel for a week or two at least."

"Isn't it expensive?"

"Not for just a couple of weeks. We'll manage." Naturally, I was the financier. Albert's dad had given him some money, which amounted to about one hundred pounds. I told him to hold on to that until he could find a job, hopefully with London Transport.

Albert got a job with London Transport quicker than either of us had imagined. He had to do some training first and they assigned him to a bus route, as conductor, from the Battersea Depot.

I was not quite so lucky with finding a house. I combed several areas of London – at least those I knew I could afford – but seemed to draw a blank on each occasion. We actually spent three weeks at the hotel in Queensway before I finally found a three-bedroom house in Southfields, close to Wimbledon Park. I loved it the moment I saw it and the price was right. Three thousand pounds and no problem with a mortgage. It had a small front garden with a privet hedge and a few rose trees, and a long, narrow back garden. It was in excellent condition, newly painted inside and out. I did not hesitate.

Albert showed some enthusiasm but he was not happy in London, even if we had lived in Buckingham Palace – that was plainly obvious. The only time he seemed to be really happy was when we made love, which we did often and passionately, and some of his fears and doubts seemed to dissipate. It was when he had to get up early on cold mornings to go to work that he became morose.

I contacted the bank in which Aunt Lucy had left the five hundred pounds for me and yes, it was there, and interest had accrued. For some reason best known to God, I had not mentioned this little nest egg to Albert, and I decided to transfer it to a different account, drawing more interest. It proved to be a life-saver.

Albert and I got married at Caxton Hall. It had always been my wish, if I were to be married in London, to do it at Caxton Hall because of the prestige and all. I dare say it boosted my ego. We had to use the address of a fellow-worker of Albert's who lived in the Westminster area, because those were the requirements. The same guy, Bert, along with my next-door neighbour, Jean, with whom I became friendly, were witnesses.

I was now Mrs Albert Wetherby. I kept repeating the name silently over and over. I felt chuffed as I posed with Albert for pictures. He looked so handsome.

Christmas, 1953, in our new home was a joyous occasion and I had never seen Albert so happy. We went cruising along Oxford Street and Regent Street to admire the Christmas lights, and then into Trafalgar Square to stand, with hundreds of others, and gaze at the huge Christmas tree, sent as a gift from Norway.

I had more reasons than one to be happy. I had just discovered, after a visit to the doctor, that I was pregnant. That made Christmas a double occasion to celebrate. Albert appeared to be overjoyed. He said he wanted a boy – like all fathers, I suppose.

I had a very difficult task looming ahead of me. I had to sit down and write the most difficult letter of my life. To Ellen and Wilfred. I wrote the letter after Christmas. I did not wish to spoil their Christmas and New Year celebrations:

Dear Mum and Dad,

This is the most difficult letter I have ever had to write, but without further preamble, I shall get straight to the point.

When I left Barbados, it was an elopement of sorts. I was not alone. I was accompanied by Albert Wetherby from the Wetherby Farm at Boston Bay. We got married recently at Caxton Hall, and I am now Mrs Albert Wetherby, and we are expecting a baby in July this year.

I know that by now your mouths have dropped open and you are shocked. I am truly sorry about that, but please understand that this is my life and I have a right to do what I please with it. I do not think I have done anything wrong – at least in the eyes of God – by marrying Albert, and although I know it will be difficult for you to do, I am begging you to accept this fact, and if possible, to give me your blessings. I am very happy and so is Albert.

Wishing you both all the very best for the New Year,

Love,
Sam

I did not expect an answer, and when one finally came, about two months later, it was from Ellen only. It was short and to the point. '*Dear Samantha*' (not 'Sam'). How could I do such a thing; my father was in a state of shock; the entire family was flabbergasted, not to mention friends and not-such-friends; practically the entire island was in an uproar; imagine how the black people were laughing; imagine how the whites were sniggering, especially all the old ladies hiding behind their fans in church; blah, blah, blah. It ended abruptly '*Your Mother*'. No love, no good wishes, and positively no acceptance of my situation or of Albert.

Then there was the letter from Gwennie, now in Australia. Had I taken leave of my senses? There were she and Richard and six-weeks-old Caroline trying to get settled in their new home in Sydney, and their lives were almost shattered by news from Barbados that I had upped and married a black boy. Who the hell was this Albert Wetherby, anyhow, and how the hell did I get myself involved with him? And to make matters ten times worse, I was going to give birth to a half-caste child who would probably have woolly hair. Good

God. Had I not almost committed myself to Tony Brownfield? On and on went the letter. *Shame and scandal in de family.*

The 'half-caste' bit sent me into fits of laughter. What a bloody nerve! What did she think her own father was? Could this really be my sister writing such crap?

I did not destroy the letters but I hid them from Albert. I could not reveal to him how pathetic my family were. As if he didn't already know.

As to Gwennie's reference to Tony, I had long since written to him, before I left Barbados, to tell him that I was in love with someone else but that I hoped we could still be friends. I had received an answer in which he expressed his profound regret and sadness but thanked me for being honest and wished me all the best. He ended off, much as Roy had, "if things go wrong, let me know." That was comforting.

Albert and I wrote a joint letter to his parents and received a reply from his mum. She wished us well and hoped that everything would go well with the birth of her grandchild. She said that the news concerning Albert and I had hit Boston Bay like a ten-ton bomb and it was all people could find to talk about from the rum shops down to the fishing boats. Mr. Wetherby was not very pleased, she revealed.

So much for outlook in Barbados – throughout the entire social spectrum. Victorian England had nothing on Barbados' narrow-mindedness and petty prejudices. They were in a class by themselves. God forgive them.

Raymond Albert Wetherby was born in July, 1954. Albert had chosen the name Raymond after his father. I wrote and asked Roy to be godfather, to which he willingly agreed. My neighbour, Jean, was one godmother and an old school friend, with whom I had kept in touch from time to time, was the other.

Interestingly, as Raymond grew, he exhibited no signs of his coloured background. He had Caucasian features except perhaps for rather full lips, and sleek, wavy brown hair. He was a handsome child and I adored him. I think Albert did too, but sad to say, I was growing increasingly uneasy about Albert's oftentimes peculiar behaviour. He seemed to be developing an attitude problem and sometimes it scared me. He appeared irritable quite often, and when I asked him questions, he answered me short.

I confided in Jean one morning, sitting in her cosy, bright-coloured kitchen, which she and her husband, Les, had decorated from ideas found in *Good Housekeeping*. It was always a pleasure to sit in Jean's kitchen and look out onto her back garden where, in the spring, daffodils and tulips grew in profusion, and a variety of flowering plants flourished in the summer. Jean loved her garden.

Jean poured some coffee, passed me a cup and then stubbed out her cigarette in a large Black & White whisky ashtray on the kitchen table, and blew the smoke through her nose. "How long has this behaviour of Albert's been going on?" she wanted to know.

"Difficult to pinpoint exactly when but I would say soon after Ray was born."

Jean nodded knowingly. "Just jealousy, probably."

"But he loves Ray."

"Yes, love, but he may feel that Ray is getting some of the affection and attention that he should be getting, know what I mean?"

"But we make love just the same as before."

Jean lit another cigarette. I wished she wouldn't smoke so much. I hated the smell of cigarette smoke. She thought for a moment. "Have you confronted him with your concerns?"

I fanned the cigarette smoke away from my face. Jean's reaction was immediate. She stubbed the newly-lit cigarette out and gave a sheepish smile. "Some day I'll give it up," she said.

"To answer your question, yes, but in a roundabout way. I've asked him if there is anything bothering him; if he is happy at work, that sort of thing."

"And?"

I hesitated. "Jean, he was annoyed. He said to me, 'Hey, girl, you giving me the third degree?' and walked out of the room."

Jean made a face. "Hmm. Don't like the sound of that. Men can be so bloody-minded at times. Know what I would do? Ignore it for a while and see what happens."

"Maybe you're right."

Jean got up and poured us some more coffee. We chatted for a while longer and then I left. Just as I was about to open my front gate, I saw the postman doing his rounds. I waited for him and he handed me two letters. One was the usual advertising junk mail and the other was from Barbados, addressed to Albert. I did not recognise the handwriting. He had already left for work so I left it on the hall table where he would see it when he came home.

I was in the kitchen, messing about between the stove and minding Ray, who was bouncing about in his high chair, waving a spoon in the air one minute and 'blowing raspberries' the next, with the baby food splattering all over his mouth, down his chin and onto the bib.

I heard the key turn in the front door lock. It was Albert. I rushed to clean up Ray's face so that his father could kiss him.

"Hi," said Albert, and going straight over to Ray, he smothered him with kisses.

I waited, just to see if he would revert to his old habit of kissing me first, which of late had become somewhat obscure, but instead I had found myself rushing forward to kiss him. Then I remembered Jean's advice. I said a quick "hi", and turned back to the stove.

"Hey! Don't I rate a kiss any more?" Albert was right behind me. I turned round and kissed him. I was on the point of saying, "I didn't think you cared", but something stopped me.

He had not seen the letter on the hall table. "There's a letter for you from Barbados. I don't recognise the handwriting."

Albert gave me a quick, pensive look and went off to get the letter. He went upstairs to the bedroom to read it.

I gave Ray his bath and put him to bed. He was a pretty good child when it came to bedtime – a few kisses, hugs, his favourite teddy, and he was off to sleep.

I was watching TV when Albert came into the living room. The look on his face was impossible to interpret. It was a mixture of anxiety and guilt. Guilt for what, though?

I was about to ask him what was the news from Barbados when he bent over and kissed me on the forehead. He sat down in the chair opposite me and leaned forward. "Um ... Sam." I looked at him. The expression on his face was one of consternation and he seemed to find it difficult to continue.

"Something wrong at home?" I asked.

He shook his head – negative, then positive. "Well, sort of. It's my mum. She wants to come over for a visit."

I looked at him in amazement. "The letter was from your mother?"

He must have suddenly remembered that I had said I did not recognise the handwriting. He glanced up quickly. This guy was definitely guilty of something.

"Well, it was written by my cousin."

"Your cousin? So why didn't your mum write herself, as she usually does?"

Albert looked angry. "You know something, Samantha? You should have been a lawyer. Questions, questions, questions." He was rubbing his hands together nervously. I wished to God I knew what was wrong. I waited.

"I'm sorry, Sam. Listen, my cousin says my mum wishes to come over but she doesn't have the money. I was wondering, could you … um … sort of lend me two hundred pounds to pay her passage?"

I thought of the money stashed in the bank that I hadn't touched. The money that dear old Aunt Lucy had left me. I had sworn never to touch it except in a case of emergency, but all other funds had been practically depleted. Albert did not know about the other five hundred pounds so where did he think I would get the money from.

I looked at him. "Where do you think I would get that kind of money, Al?"

He fidgeted. "You mean all your money is used up?"

"Practically." I thought for a minute. I was fond of Mrs Wetherby and perhaps she wanted to see her grandson. I softened. "Well, I suppose I could scrape up two hundred quid, but it would leave the bank account at zero."

Albert looked like a lost child. He got up and came over to me and put his arms around me. Something he hadn't done for ages. I guess it went to my head. I loved the guy like crazy.

"Please, Sam. I swear I'll pay you back as soon as I can. A guy at work owes me fifty pounds for a start."

Charming. A guy at work owes him fifty quid, when we are barely eking out a living!

Next morning, Ray and I set off for the bank in Southfields. Jean went with us. She had no children and she loved pushing Ray in his stroller and sharing 'motherhood' with me. Whenever Albert and I wanted to go out, Jean was a natural baby-sitter.

Southfields had a village atmosphere yet it was where working-class, middle-class, and I daresay a sprinkle of upper-class met in and around the shops, which weren't many but were adequate. A couple of banks, a chemist, a butcher, greengrocer, tobacconist – all the essential shops – as well as an antique shop which Roy would have loved. There was also the Underground train on the District Line which in actual fact, at that point, was above ground between Wimbledon and Earls Court.

Bank transaction completed, we visited one or two shops for purchases before strolling over to Wimbledon Park. Ray loved to see the ducks in the lake. He was now eleven months old, and between Jean and I, we spent hours trying to get him to walk.

"You say his mum's coming over for a visit?" asked Jean.

"Yes. He got a letter – oddly enough not from his mother, but from a cousin – expressing the wish that the old lady could visit and meet her grandson."

Jean made a face. It was difficult to interpret the expression. "A cousin? Why not his mum herself – doesn't she write sometimes?"

I looked at Jean. "That's the puzzling thing. And I'll tell you this – I had some reservations about withdrawing that two hundred quid."

"Why?"

I shrugged. "Don't know. However, the proof of the pudding will be in the eating. I mean, we'll soon see when she arrives, won't we. She can't be with us for another six weeks or so, by the time she gets the money and gets booked up – most likely on one of the Italian liners that ply between Barbados and Southampton every fortnight."

Jean stopped in her tracks. "How's he going to get the money to her then? Surely he should have asked you to send a bank draft, or something."

"Never thought of that. I guess he's going to buy a draft himself with the cash." Why were we in so much doubt, I wondered.

The corners of Jean's mouth turned down. "Yeah. I suppose." She shrugged and we continued on our stroll, with Ray squirming in his stroller when he saw the ducks on the lake. It was a beautiful day for June in England. Warm and sunny and there were lots of middle-aged and elderly folk enjoying the sunshine in the park, some playing bowls on the green, others feeding the ducks or just strolling. Nannies were pushing babies in prams – obviously from the more affluent homes up on Wimbledon Hill. Older children were in school. Two or three ducks took off from the water like seaplanes and landed in the bushes on a little island on the far side of the lake. Ray clapped his hands.

Jean and I, taking turns to push Ray's stroller, walked around the park for a while longer, sharing jokes and experiences in life. It turned out that I was forced to do most of the talking, because Jean was always fascinated with my descriptions of Barbados. She would sigh and say, "Oh, you lucky thing. Wish I could get to Barbados on holiday. I would spend all day on the beach and dance calypsos at your Club Morgan at night. What could be better!"

"I don't know, Jean, Club Morgan is nice but it smacks of South Africa and the Deep South, USA, you know? All whites. No black people allowed."

"Yeah. That would bother me. Why is it like that?"

"It will change one day, you wait and see. It has to." I wasn't sure that I believed my own words, but we live in hope.

"Hey, listen, Jean. I've been thinking. As soon as Ray is just over a year, I think I'll look for a job. What do you think?"

Jean punched me playfully on the arm. "Go on! You're not, are you? What for? You need the money?"

"Yes. My bank reserves are dwindling, and although Albert's wages keep us going, we could do better if I were working."

"Well, if it means I get to keep Ray while you're at work, I'll agree."

I stopped and looked at her hard. "Jean, God bless you. What would I do without you? I wouldn't even think of leaving him with anyone else, if you would have him." She assured me she would love that and we strolled back home.

10

Six months after I gave Albert the two hundred quid to bring his mum over to England, there was still no sign of her. Christmas was upon us. Perhaps she will turn up shortly, I thought.

It was a waste of time asking Albert questions. He either sulked, shouted at me and then apologised, or said he did not know why she had not come. Yes, he had sent off the two hundred pound bank draft, which was the approximate equivalent of nine hundred and sixty Barbados dollars. The fare between Barbados and Britain was between four hundred and six hundred Barbados dollars, depending upon the shipping line. What was the problem?

"Has your mum written to say anything?" I asked him one evening. He glanced up from the newspaper in which he was completing the football pools. "Isn't that a stupid question? I mean, you're home when the mail comes, you would have seen a letter from her." He shook the newspaper and got on with the pools.

I shut up and watched a programme on TV. I was frustrated. Come to think of it, I had changed a lot without even realising it. I had obviously matured, having a husband and an eighteen-month old son, and I was beginning to learn a lot more about myself than previously. I think I was becoming a new *me*.

I had more or less taken things for granted before, and had been content to let the chips fall where they might. Whereas I had led a fairly pampered existence before, I now found myself in a highly responsible position. It even surprised me to recall how I had 'taken over' when coaxing Albert to travel to England with me; I had been the one to do the house-hunting and to go through the legal procedures of house purchase, arranging for a mortgage, buying furniture and all other details. And Albert? Well, he found a job for himself and that was about all he did. From home to work and work to home, coming home quite late some Friday nights when he was on the day shift, after 'having a drink with the boys'.

On his days off, he seldom wanted to go walking in the park with Ray and me. He was 'too tired', he said. I had thought that when Ray started to walk – which he did one morning out of the blue over at Jean's house, when he had just turned one year old – Albert would have enjoyed a stroll in the park with him, even if he wasn't into 'feeding ducks in a lake', as he moaned. It reminded him of his cows and other farmyard animals back home.

"Are you homesick?" I once asked him.

He did not hesitate. "What do you think? Of course I am. Here we are, stuck in this cold, mouldy country, far away from the beach and sea, and ..." he did not finish the sentence but left the room in a huff.

He had twice assured me that I would get my money back even if his mother did not come over. He would do some overtime if necessary. This never materialised and I decided to write off the loan. I was sure I would never get the money back. I just wanted to know what had become of it. It was not in his mother's character to take money, especially knowing it had been a loan from me to be used for a passage to England, and then use it for something else without writing to explain. The whole thing was baffling and it bothered me.

"I don't like the sound of that," said Jean when I revealed the problem to her. She kept asking when my mother-in-law was coming, and when by Christmas the old lady hadn't appeared, Jean buttonholed me while we were having coffee in my kitchen one morning. She asked where was Mrs Wetherby, and I admitted that we did not know and had not heard from her.

"Nope, don't like the sound of that at all," she repeated.

"Well, neither do I but what can I do?"

"Write to your mother-in-law and ask her when she's coming."

I jumped around in my chair. "Are you crazy? You want Albert to kill me?"

"Don't see why he should unless he's hiding something."

I looked at her. "Hiding something like what? If one of his parents is ill and in need of hospitalisation or expensive medical treatment or some such thing, why would he lie and say his mum was coming over? He should know I would be suspicious when she doesn't turn up."

"Exactly." Jean gave a little shiver. "Gives me the willies, it does. Something's not right."

"You can say that again."

Jean sipped her coffee. She was about to take a cigarette out of a packet in her pocket when I held up my hand. "God's truth, I forgot!" she said, quickly replacing the packet in her pocket, and we both said in the same breath, "No smoking in this house!" and laughed.

"At least we can have a bit of a giggle," Jean said, and was about to say something else when the kitchen door opened and Albert stood in the doorway. Neither of us had heard him come through the front door down the hallway and I nearly fainted. I wondered if he had been listening outside the door and if so, for how long.

Jean said, "Hello, Albert."

I said, "You gave us a fright. How come you're not at work?"

"Hello, Jean. Could I have a cup of coffee, Sam?"

I got up and put the kettle on. Albert put down his shoulder bag, took off his heavy coat, hung it up and sat down at the table.

"Where's Ray?" he asked.

"In his bedroom, fast asleep."

"Is he okay? Chicken pox is going around."

"Far as I know he's okay."

Albert did not give any sign that he had overheard our chat. He must have realised that an explanation was necessary and said, "Came home early because I'm not feeling so good." Then he glanced at Jean. "So this is what you two do all day – drink coffee and gossip."

Jean sent me a quick look. Always one to rise to the occasion, she said, "That's right, love. We know everything about the neighbours and their carryings-on."

I put a steaming cup of coffee in front of Albert. He did not intend to linger in the kitchen with the womenfolk. He took up the cup, excused himself and went upstairs.

After Jean left, I went up to the bedroom to see if Albert wanted some aspirin. No, he was okay. He had taken two aspirins just before leaving work. He called me over to the bed where he was lying in his underpants and a sweater.

"Come over here. I feel horny," he said.

I stared at him, wondering if he had been drinking. Our love-making these days boiled down to once a month – if that – and mostly at night. This was not quite midday and here was Albert saying he felt horny. The longer I lived with this man, the less I understood him.

I went over to the bed. "I thought you weren't feeling well."

He grabbed me. "The aspirin must have given me a high!"

We made passionate love for the first time in many months. I did not smell alcohol on his breath but I kept smelling a very faint whiff of strange perfume and it was not men's cologne. I said nothing for fear of angering him. But I did not forget it.

As for Albert, as soon as he finished he rolled away from me and went fast asleep. I could hear Ray murmuring away to himself in his bedroom so I got up reluctantly and went to fix some lunch.

Albert's strange behaviour became stranger. He was on the day shift for a long time and he had taken to going out at night after his evening meal. Sometimes he came home around ten thirty, other times it was more like two in the morning. Could he be gambling, I wondered. West Indian men have a habit of playing dominoes well into the wee hours of morning. I was in a quandary. If I asked questions, I was accused of 'harassing' him.

After that last surprise love-making session, he reverted to his old self – sometimes two months would go by before he 'felt horny', and even then the act was far from passionate, with few words, and more like a 'wham-bam-thank-you-ma'am' affair.

I got up the courage a few times to ask him what was going on and of course he snapped at me, "Nothing. Nothing is going on. I told you, I get together with some boys from work and we have a few drinks and slap some dominoes."

"Then one of the boys must wear lipstick," I said on one occasion, bravely holding up one of his handkerchiefs which had some faint lipstick marks. "And he must kiss you goodnight."

Albert spun around and snatched the handkerchief from my hand. "Where did you get this?"

"Christ, Albert, I am the bloody slave who washes your clothes, remember?"

Albert appeared floored by such an outburst from me. I had just about had it up to my ears and I was furious.

"This is not lipstick, Samantha," he said, examining the handkerchief.

That was an insult to my intelligence but I laughed. "So what is it then – pink Scotch Mist?"

Albert flounced out of the room, slamming the door.

The truth was beginning to sink into my befuddled brain. My husband, whom I adored, was obviously having an affair. I was so devastated that I did not even wish to tell Jean.

I thought back about Albert and I, when we first met in Barbados, how we fell in love – or so I thought – and how romantic it was; our secret meetings in Holetown; our exciting, but innocent meetings on the beach at night, behind the sea grape trees. It was all so wonderful, and I had truly thought that Albert loved me as much as I loved him.

Alas, the crystal ball was shattering – because that's how it appeared to me now – and there was pain in my heart. What had gone wrong? Was it my fault? Had I dragged Albert away from the security of his real home – his beloved farm at Boston Bay? He had been reluctant at the idea of going to England at first, and then I remembered how he had suddenly changed his mind and was almost anxious to travel.

I did talk to Jean in the end. There was no one else to turn to. Forget Ellen and Wilfred; forget Gwennie. It is true that Ellen had written to me a few times, and so had Gwennie, and I had always replied. Their letters were almost formal – essays of their respective happenings, ending with the hope that everything was okay with me and please give Ray kisses and hugs. Not a word about Albert, of course. It was as if he didn't exist.

I had also received a letter or two from Roy – always cheerful and full of gossip. I always replied to Roy immediately. In one letter he informed me that Tony had married 'that dreadful painted creature, Greta'.

I was flabbergasted, and yes, I felt a twinge of jealousy. Fancy Tony marrying Greta! But I was too wrapped up in my own affairs to give it much thought. To each his own.

Jean had made her usual face when I told her of my suspicions. "Blimey, they all do it, don't they. Bloody men!"

"You don't mean that Les has ..."

"Course he has. It happened about five years ago. They met at a party and things happened. Probably had something to do with us not being able to have kids." She shrugged. "Who knows."

"How did you find out?"

"Same way you did. Lipstick on shirt collars."

"You tackled him about it?"

"Of course. Look, Sam, not that I like making comparisons but Les is not like your Albert. Les admitted it but he said it was over and it had only lasted a few months. He begged me to forgive him, which I did. Since then, as far as I know, there has never been another incident."

"So what do I do now?"

We were in the park and it was summer again. Jean blew cigarette smoke through her nose and watched some ducks take off from the water and soar into the blue sky. We had left Ray with Jean's mother, who was visiting, because he had a cold and was all stuffed up and sniffling.

Jean looked at me. "Not much you can do, love. Especially as Albert is behaving the way he is. He's insulting your intelligence, that's what. Tell me something. Are all West Indian men like that?"

"Like what?"

"I mean, if they have affairs, do they deny it outright although you have evidence?"

I was baffled. I honestly did not know the answer. I could only judge by my father, and I smiled as I thought of the possibility of Wilfred having an extra-marital affair. It was unthinkable. I told Jean I hadn't a clue. Why would West Indian men be any different to other men? I daresay I knew in my heart of hearts that there was some substance in Jean's remark.

Sometime in September 1956, and roughly one month after my chat with Jean, I was vacuuming the carpet on the stairs and singing a Country and Western song when the doorbell rang. It was a warm day and Ray was in the back garden in his playpen.

I opened the door and there stood this brown-skinned young lady, dressed smartly in a light sweater and skirt with a raincoat over her arm. She looked at me with what I could only describe as hostility. All of a sudden I recognised her. She was Albert's 'cousin' – the one who had been on the bicycle way back when in Barbados.

"Are you Mrs Wetherby?"

I nodded. "Yes. And you are?"

She hesitated. I waited. She looked down at the ground. Then she looked me full in the eyes and said, "I am Sheila."

I waited for more. Her last name. Whatever. Nothing more appeared to be forthcoming.

"Sheila? Sheila who?" I was on the point of saying, "Albert's cousin?" but something stopped me.

"Look, could I come in and talk to you?" she asked.

I motioned her in and we went into the living room. I invited her to sit down but she stood by the empty fireplace and leaned on the mantlepiece. She gazed around the room. I could not escape the feeling of hostility emanating from her and I was becoming uncomfortable.

"The name Sheila don't mean nothing to you?"

Uneducated girl, this one. "I'm afraid it doesn't."

"Well it should. Albert should have tell you about me. He is my man."

I stared at the girl. I felt as if I were in a vacuum – out in space. Then I went numb. I couldn't move or speak. I was stuck in the chair, mesmerised by her words.

The girl laughed. "I see he ain't tell you nothing."

When finally I found my voice, I said foolishly, "You are not Albert's cousin?"

She laughed, and then within the wink of an eye, the hostile look was back.

"So that is what he tell you? That I am his cousin? The bastard! Where he is, by the way?"

I suddenly got mad. I stood up. "You come into my house, telling me my husband is your man, and have the unmitigated gall to ask me where he is?" I motioned her towards the open door. "I want you out of here – *now*."

She moved slowly towards the door and when she reached the hallway, she shouted up the stairs, "Albert, come down here, you lying dog!"

I pulled open the front door and shoved the girl out, hissing at her, "Albert is not at home, he's at work, you little bitch." I slammed the front door in her face.

After she had gone, I went out to the back garden and brought Ray in. I put him in the playpen in the living room and turned on the TV to amuse him while I fled upstairs to the bedroom, threw myself across the bed and sobbed my heart out. My lovely world had crashed around me. I was right – it had just been a crystal ball.

When finally I pulled myself together, I realised I would have to confront Albert. I knew damned well that the girl Sheila would, and Albert would be waiting for the explosion from me. I was in a no-win situation. Damned if you do, damned if you don't. I would have to try and keep my cool.

Albert did not come home that evening. I suppose he couldn't face me. He arrived home the next evening around six thirty, looking thoroughly dishevelled. His face was set up in a scowl – a defence mechanism. That meant I would have to attack immediately.

"Albert, it's time for a showdown," I said.

He scowled at me. "Showdown about what?"

"You know damned well about *whom* – not what. About Sheila."

"Sheila? My cousin, Sheila?"

"Jesus Christ, Albert, come off it!"

He shouted at me, "Come off *what,* Samantha? What are you moaning about now?"

I couldn't believe this guy. But before I could say anything else, he turned on his heel and marched out of the room, looking over his shoulder with this parting shot: "You have a vivid imagination and you're always accusing me of things I know nothing about." He took a half step backwards and his chin jutted out when he said, "You forget that I gave up my home in Barbados to live in this god-forsaken place with you." Then he stamped off.

I don't know which hurt me the most – Sheila's revelation or Albert's reaction.

Life goes on. Life gets better for some and life gets worse for some. Life got worse for me. There was a complete breakdown in the relationship between Albert and me. We were barely speaking to each other and he continued to deny an affair with Sheila, or any other woman for that matter, despite the lipstick on handker-chiefs, shirt collars and shirtsleeves. My imagination, he said.

Who was this man? Surely he was not the Albert I had known in Barbados. Then, Kellie's previous warnings suddenly surfaced. This was obviously the man that Kellie knew. Unfortunately, I still loved him, and if he had talked to me and we had been able to work things out, I would have forgiven him.

Jean was stunned when I told her. Not so much because he was having an affair but because of his peculiar behaviour. She did not understand it. It was un-British – not cricket – and she did not understand un-British behaviour. As far as she was concerned, when you got caught out, you came clean, confessed, apologised, promised to behave in future, and that was how the cookie was supposed to crumble.

It never rains but it pours. A week or two later – during which time Albert and I were barely polite to each other – the postman very kindly dropped a bombshell through my letterbox. A letter from the girl, Sheila. Since she was not allowed to come to my house, she said, she would let me know in writing what was going on.

She explained that she and Albert had been lovers in Barbados and I had 'snatched' him away from her. She was actually two months pregnant for him before he left Barbados, and he knew it. (Now I understood his sudden anxiety to leave!)

After her baby daughter was born, she wrote and asked Albert to send some money for her passage to England as she wanted to be with him. He sent the money, and here she is and here she intends to stay. She also intends to have Albert back, so I had better not try to stop her.

I sat for a very long time in the kitchen, with the letter in my hand. I felt quite numb. My brain refused to function. Whatever I did for at least half an hour after that was purely mechanical. Ray had had his breakfast and was out in the garden playing with his toys. I made the beds and tidied up the house as best I could, trying not to think of the cruel blow fate had dealt me. I would have to find a solution. But not right now.

My mood swiftly changed later that evening, as soon as I heard the key in the front door. My hackles were raised. This was going to be the showdown to beat all showdowns, no matter the consequences.

Some people can calmly rationalise situations and deal with them accordingly. I am not endowed with such virtues. I become irrational and let off steam, which was exactly what I did as soon as Albert stepped through the door.

I flung the letter at him and said, "Get out of this one, if you can!"

He was taken aback and for a second there was a glimmer of fear in his face. He took the letter and went upstairs to the bedroom. I followed him.

His face paled when he read the letter but he kept his compo-sure. He looked at me and opened his eyes questioningly. "So?"

"What do you mean, *so*? You are reacting as if it were a 'Dear Jane, how's tricks' letter. I want an explanation from *you*. I've got one from her."

Albert came towards me almost as if he were tempting me to hit him, which was exactly what I felt like doing. He tore the letter to shreds. "I have nothing to explain to you. *Nothing*. Do you hear? I am a big grown-up man, not a child. Neither am I a prisoner." He came very close to me and shook his finger in my face. "You know your trouble? You and that Jean next door are getting together against me, and I am sick and fed up with it."

I slapped his finger away and immediately he drew back his hand and slapped me hard in the face. Not satisfied with that, like a shark tasting blood, he hauled off and fetched me another blow, more like a cuff, which centred on my right eye. I reeled back and stumbled. Ray, who was in the room watching the fracas, screamed and ran to me. I snatched him up and fled from the room.

Next day I had a proper shiner. I went over to Jean's house with Ray in tow. She was in the middle of her housework but when she saw me, she dropped everything and ran to me.

"Oh, my God!" She held me at arm's length and stared at my eye and swollen cheek. "Albert?"

I nodded. "Come." She led me into the kitchen and put the kettle on for some coffee. We put Ray out in the back garden where we could keep an eye on him through the kitchen window.

"First thing, love, you see your doctor."

"Oh God, Jean, I don't want him to know …"

"You belt up and listen to me! You have to think ahead. You may very well need evidence. Listen, love, stop thinking of the 'old' Albert that you knew in Barbados. He's gone. What's more, he was make-believe, okay? This is the *real* Albert you're dealing with and he is *bad news*. I don't know what is his problem – prob-ably having to deal with two women and two babies, and he can't handle it. You can't solve anything by talking to him because he is unreasonable and doesn't want to know. So what it boils down to is less talk and more action."

Jean, Ray and I went to the doctor. Jean kept Ray while I went into the doctor's office. He couldn't help much with the black eye except to give me a cream to rub on the lid and my cheek, and some tablets. But he recorded everything and was very sympathetic. The police were more professional in their approach. They asked a lot of questions and took a statement. Did I wish to press charges or take the matter further? Not at this stage, I said. I just wanted it recorded.

I overheard one policeman murmuring to another, "These bloody West Indians – always banging up their wives and women-folk." Jean and I exchanged glances.

The sergeant informed me that should it happen again, I should let them know immediately and we would take it from there. He smiled at Ray and ruffled his hair. "Good-looking kid," he said.

11

THERE is a lot of water under the bridge now. Stagnant, dirty water, I call it. Things happened very fast after that first bashing from Albert. I had difficulty believing that this was reality. It was more like a horrible nightmare in which I was caught up in a whirlwind vortex. Jean was right – gone indeed was the original, or make-believe, Albert.

I started blaming myself. I should never have dragged him away from Barbados. I took him out of his element. When I became friendly with Jean, I had hoped that Albert would at least join in the social relationship and have something in common with Les. I know that Les had hoped for this too, because once or twice when he had been home and I was visiting Jean, he had expressed such a wish. "Hey, Sam, tell that husband of yours to give me a shout some Saturday evening and we'll go have a drink at the pub."

Les actually came over to our house one Saturday night, looking for Albert, but Albert had already gone out to have a drink with the boys – or so he said.

It was not to say that Jean and Les were snobs, or even middle-class people. They were a working-class couple, and given Albert's own background, he should have had no difficulty making friends with Les. Granted, Les may have had a better education, but he would never have talked down to Albert – he would have found a mutual level because that was the type of man Les was. Neither he nor Jean had any hang-ups as regards colour and class so that was not a problem.

Since living in London, Albert had simply chosen to stick to his West Indian friends working with London Transport and that was that. One friend, in particular, a very dark Barbadian by the name of Eric, used to visit our home occasionally. He was a pretty decent guy and always very polite to me.

When things went wrong between Albert and I, Eric appeared at the door one Sunday, looking for Albert. Albert, as usual, was not home. He seldom was, since Sheila had appeared on the scene.

I invited Eric in for a cup of coffee and I tried to induce him into talking about Albert, but, as pleasant and sympathetic as he was, his lips were sealed. I shouldn't have been surprised, knowing how West Indian men stick together, especially when it comes to marital affairs. They are quite unable to understand what the 'fuss' is all about; it is understood and accepted among them that men, married or not, must have more than one woman. A man would be some sort of freak to stick to one woman for a lifetime, and at best, that woman would be a very selfish person!

Eric did, however, drop a few remarks which homed in on my ever-extended antennae when trying to pick him about Albert. "You must give Albert a chance, Sam. He is a bit mixed up at the moment. A lot of us Barbadians living in Britain have, to a certain extent, settled down – always with the intention of returning to Barbados, of course – but your Albert has not. He misses the farm and going fishing with his brother, and he hates the cold."

I nodded in agreement, and the guilt feelings were back. Guilt over persuading Albert to leave Barbados. On the other hand, I hadn't bound and gagged him and shoved him on the ship and, after all, he had been enthusiastic after the first initial doubts.

I knew I wouldn't get any more out of Eric that day or any other day. Unless he had designs on me and wanted to get me in bed, he certainly wasn't going to enlighten me any further. I was glad that he refrained from any such desires.

I was seething with rage over my two hundred pounds that Albert had so blatantly lied about. I wanted it back and I told him so in no uncertain terms. I lost my temper one morning when he just gave me a disdainful look and continued combing his hair and admiring himself in the mirror. I stupidly went up to him, grabbed his arm and shook him. He whirled on me, gave me a tremendous shove and sent me sprawling across the room. I fell, hitting my head on the tiled side of the fireplace. Not satisfied with that, he came over and kicked me in the side. He left me lying there and ran downstairs out of the house, slamming the front door as he went.

I lay there for a while, hurting all over – both physically and mentally – and then I pulled myself up slowly and sat holding my head, which felt as if it had been squeezed in a vice. Time for action, I thought. Kid gloves are off. This is doctor time, police time, lawyer time. What love I had left for Albert was dying, and in its place hatred was settling in. They say love and hatred are closely related.

I took Ray over to Jean. My side hurt and I was limping. My left ear was redder than a cherry and there was a swelling on the upper jaw. Jean just took me in her arms, hugged me and began to cry. Crying time was over for me.

"Keep Ray for me while I go to the doctor, Jean."

"No way. We all go together."

"Not this time, Jean. Let me do this on my own. I'll put on a scarf to hide the marks on my face." She reluctantly let me go.

The doctor was furious. "You get away from that man before he kills you, you hear me? Go straight to the police when I've finished with you, and then get yourself a lawyer." He must have read my thoughts.

The police took the statement and I signed it. "I'm going to look for a lawyer now," I informed the sergeant. He walked me to the station door. "Sure you're all right, love?" I nodded.

Back at Jean's house, we looked up law firms in the telephone directory and picked out one along Merton Road, Wandsworth. Jean had a telephone so we made the call from her house, and I was given an appointment for the following week.

Solicitor's offices are always stuffy and this one was no exception. I was ushered into Mr Hanson's office by a smartly dressed secretary.

Mr Hanson stood up from his swivel chair behind the desk and shook my hand. He was very old-fashioned looking, probably in his mid-sixties, grey hair, balding on the top, and his nose supported a pair of bifocal eye-glasses. He wore a conservative grey pin-striped suit with a pin-striped tie. He couldn't have looked more like a lawyer if he'd tried.

We talked for almost an hour. Well, I did. I told him I wanted a divorce. He asked many questions which I thought at the time were irrelevant, but later realised that the man was no fool!

When I had completed my exposé, Mr Hanson gazed at me thoughtfully, before he said, "Now. Let me get this straight. Your father is a doctor, you were educated at a boarding-school in this country. That puts you in a middle-class bracket. Your husband's family are small farmers." He paused for a moment, then cleared his throat and continued, "Is he black, by any chance?"

"Coloured. Mixed blood, in other words."

He must have thought I objected to the word 'black', for he quickly said, "The reason I ask that, my dear, is because our firm is experiencing similar situations to yours – assault and battery – on English wives of West Indian men. However, most of the wives are working-class women. Your situation is interesting, from the point of view that here we have a woman from a middle-class family, married to a man from a working-class family, and we also have the element of colour."

Was this man a bloody psychiatrist, or what? I shifted uneasily in my chair. What was he leading up to?

He leaned forward. "I see you have applied for Legal Aid."

"Yes. Is that a problem?"

"Oh, no. Not at all, that was just by the way." He cleared his throat again and launched forth into some rather interesting dialogue, to which I listened carefully. I still hadn't completely grasped his need for delving into family backgrounds. He said we had a strong case for adultery, mental and physical cruelty – the works. The only problem being that the daily tabloids, always sniffing around the courts with some very sharp journalists, could easily pick up on the distasteful details – 'white, middle-class woman married to a black working-class West Indian who commits adultery and indulges in wife-beating.'

I interjected. "But I am a West Indian too."

"Ah, yes, but you're *white*, and middle-class! Don't get me wrong, Mrs Wetherby, I am not sitting in judgement. I am only telling you the angle the newspapers would go for."

I took a deep breath. "I'm not white, Mr Hanson."

"I beg your pardon?"

"My grandmother was a half-caste lady."

Mr Hanson pondered this last bit of information. He rubbed his chin, fixed his eyeglasses, and said, "Are you going to tell that to the newspapers?"

He floored me with that question. What the hell sort of question was that anyhow? I mean, you don't walk around shouting from the rooftops, "my grandmother was coloured", or "my aunt Bessie died of cancer" – that sort of thing.

I shrugged. "Not necessarily."

"Exactly. To all intents and purposes, my dear, you are white. Please forgive me for being personal, but you … ah …" (clears his throat) "have no characteristic coloured features. No one glancing at you would think to themselves, '*there goes a coloured lady*'. Do you understand what I mean? To newspaper journalists, you would be white and middle-class. Even your accent and the way you speak is middle-class. It would most certainly hit the Wandsworth Borough News. You know that there is tremendous class distinction in this country. The journalists will work on the theory that their readers will exclaim, '*serve her right – she should never have married beneath her, and worse, to a black man.*' That will be their fodder. Do you understand what I am trying to say?"

I sighed. I understood only too well. Class, class, class. Colour, colour, colour. Will it ever be any different ?

"Mr Hanson, are you saying you do not wish to take my case?"

Mr. Hanson rocked back in his chair. "Good Lord, no! Of course I'll take the case. However, I am merely pointing out the worst scenario should you wish to proceed with adultery and all the rest."

"What is the alternative?"

He scratched his balding head. "Well, we could go for desertion under duress. Mental cruelty. You say the house is yours. Can you prove that?"

I gave him the rundown on the house and how I purchased it, in detail. He said that I would probably have to sell in the end because in equity, the house was the family home, and it was shared equally between Albert and me. If it were to be sold, we would each have an equal share of the proceeds. That was how the law worked.

"But he never put a cent towards the purchase."

Mr Hanson shook his head. "Doesn't matter. It is presumed that he helped to pay off the mortgage, as he is working. Also, if he did any interior or exterior decorating, and in other words, put manual labour into the house. That sort of thing."

I thought it was grossly unfair. I told Mr Hanson I would go home and think it over and then let him know whether or not I wanted to proceed.

Less than a week after I had been to see Mr Hanson, I was sitting at home one night watching TV. Ray was asleep in his room.

Albert was not at home. All of a sudden, I heard shouting outside the house. I looked out and there was this car, a Hillman Minx, in the middle of the avenue with its engine running and park lights on. A black man was in the driver's seat and a woman was leaning through the backseat window gesticulating. It looked like Sheila, but I couldn't be sure. She yelled at the top of her voice, "Samantha Wetherby, I have your husband here with me. He is my man. Let him go, you white bitch!" I could make out someone else in the front passenger seat. The car's engine roared and it shot off up the road. I barely had time to wonder what the neighbours thought before it was back again with more shouting and with what in Barbados is called 'standpipe brawling' behaviour.

I wanted to call the police but had no phone and I knew that Jean and Les were out. I grabbed my coat quickly and started to run up the avenue to the telephone kiosk. I heard a car approaching as I ran. Looking back, I saw it was the Hillman Minx and it was coming straight at me. It swerved just as I ran into the phone booth. As it passed, I saw Albert sitting in the front passenger seat, laughing his head off, and Sheila in the back seat, rocking back and forth, screaming with laughter. I did not recognise the driver except that I knew it was not Eric.

I realised with the clarity that comes to one in such a dilemma, that they were out to kill me. This was action time again. I simply had to get to the Police Station, but Ray was at home alone.

Without hesitation, I ran back down the avenue and banged on the front door of one of the neighbours across from my house. I had met her once or twice over at Jean's house for coffee. She was Irish.

The door opened and I threw myself at her. "Mary, for God's sake, help me. Do you have a phone? I need the police urgently."

Her husband, who had heard the commotion, came out of the living room. Briefly I told them what had happened and immediately he said, "I've got a car. I'll run you down to Garratt Lane Police Station. Go fetch Ray and leave him with Mary."

On the way to the station, he told me he had witnessed the incident when the car had stopped opposite my house and the woman in the back seat was yelling.

"Bloody savages. Worse than the bleeding IRA!" he expostulated. I was thinking neither of 'savages', nor of the IRA at that moment.

I was in a state of shock when we reached the police station, and the sergeant jumped up from behind his desk and helped me into a chair. He ordered a constable to bring me a cup of tea. When I calmed down, I related the tale. The police had told my neighbour he could return home as they would look after me.

About twenty minutes later, I was escorted home in a police car with two officers. They offered to come into the house to make sure everything was okay.

The two officers and I were greatly surprised when we entered the living room, for there was Albert, calmly sitting watching TV, drinking a beer as if nothing had happened. He looked at the two officers and boldly asked them what they were doing in *his* house. But I detected fear in his voice.

The officers looked at me. They were puzzled. Was I absolutely sure I had seen Albert in the car? I would stake my life on it, I said. Furthermore, my neighbour, the Irishman, had also seen him in the car.

One of the officers said to Albert, "You've been watching TV all evening?"

"What's it to you? You can't come in here and start questioning me without my permission." He gave me a vicious look. "And Samantha, where is Ray?"

We ignored his question and the officers exchanged glances. Again, one of them said, "Sir, could you tell us what programme you were watching half an hour ago, and what was on before that?"

Albert was furious. He stood up and ordered them out of the house. "I know my rights, you know."

One officer said, "We have a report from your wife that you were in a car with two other people and the driver of the car tried to run her down."

Albert said, "Officers, my wife has a vivid imagination. Now, please leave."

The policemen explained that they had no alternative because it was the family home. However, they suggested that I take the child and go spend the night with a neighbour if I was scared. Before they left, I went across the road to fetch Ray, but Mary kindly offered to let him spend the rest of the night, as he was fast asleep.

Whether or not Albert had been scared off by the presence of the police, I don't know, for he was quiet after that, and spent the night probably on the sofa in the living room because he did not come upstairs. I waited until I heard Jean and Les come home, then I sneaked out of the house and went next door where I spent the rest of the night. None of us slept.

Les was livid. He was all for going over to my house and giving Albert the thrashing of his life, but Jean and I said that would only make matters worse. We would leave it in the hands of the police and Mr Hanson.

12

THE Decree Absolute came through in January 1958. The house had been sold for four thousand five hundred pounds, and the proceeds divided equally between Albert and me. I had moved out in 1957, and so had he. He went to live openly with Sheila and their daughter. I had been awarded sole custody of Ray, with visiting rights for Albert.

I found myself a small, two-bedroom flat over by Wandsworth Common, and I secured a job as secretary to a professor at Battersea College of Technology. I bought myself a second-hand Morris Minor coupé for one hundred and fifty pounds. Good little car. She could have done with a paint job but she had a fantastic little engine. Never let me down – fill her up with petrol, water and oil, and she kept going. I used it for work, dropping Ray off at the day nursery and picking him up on evenings.

On warm sunny Sundays during the summer, I risked driving to Littlehampton, near Worthing, where there was a sandy beach. Ray thoroughly enjoyed frisking around in the sand, building sand castles and doing all the other things that children do at the beach.

Jean died. I was devastated by that tremendous blow. It was discovered that she was riddled with cancer. They gave her six months to live. She lived four months. After that I found myself very much alone with Ray. My beloved friend was gone. Both Ray and I loved her and he kept asking me, "Where has Auntie Jean gone? Why did she die?" All I could tell him was that Jesus had called her and that her spirit was still with us. Of course he did not understand this. He missed his darling Auntie Jean and he wanted her back.

Jean was cremated at Streatham Crematorium and there was a small funeral service which I attended. I was grief-stricken. As if there hadn't been enough disappointment and sorrow in my life, now I had to face this. I thought God must have been punishing me.

Les was completely traumatised. He told me that Jean's mum and dad had invited him to go and stay with them in St Ives, Cornwall. They ran a greengrocer's shop there and, if he wanted, he could live with them and help them run the shop. He got along well with them and they loved him as a son. So Les sold the house and went off to St Ives, taking Jean's ashes in a beautiful urn with him. Every year he sent a Christmas card to Ray and me.

Ray started school in September 1959, when he was five years old. Oh, what a little beauty he was – so handsome and a proper little charmer. Everyone loved him.

I more or less withdrew into a private little world of my own. Oddly enough, my sad experiences had a profound effect on my religious beliefs. Instead of *losing* faith and blaming God for my 'punishment' as I seemed to do at first – especially after Jean died – my faith deepened. I talked to God regularly. I thanked him daily for Ray; I also thanked him for bringing Jean into my life when I most needed her; I thanked him for opening my eyes to a lot of things I would never otherwise have been aware of. I knew now that these things are sent to try us. You learn from your experiences, as bitter as they may be. Into each life some rain must fall. Inevitably one matures from these experiences.

Albert came to visit Ray about once every six months. Once he brought his daughter, Sandra, who was one year older than Ray. She was a quiet, morose child and somehow I felt sorry for her.

I no longer hated Albert. That passion had died and in its place numbness had developed. I honestly did not care whether or not he existed, or how he existed. I knew that he and Sheila lived in Tufnell Park as I had been given the address by the Court. I never made any attempt to contact them. Albert had been ordered to help support Ray but he seldom did, and I got fed up putting him in Court so I managed to pay my flat rent and utilities and Ray and I scraped by. I could not afford a telephone, but the landlady, who lived in the large ground floor flat, allowed me to use hers if it was urgent. She was a pleasant soul, and she adored Ray.

"Is Uncle Les dead too?" Ray asked me one day.

"No, my love, he is very much alive, and living in Cornwall. In his last Christmas card he invited us to go visit him and Auntie Jean's mum and dad. Perhaps we can go for a week next summer. Would you like that?"

He nodded vigorously. Then he thought for a minute. "Where is Cornwall? Is it near Barbados?" I had told Ray so much about Barbados that he thought it was the only other place in the world.

I got out my atlas and showed him where Cornwall was, just as I had shown him where Barbados was. "If we don't go there, we'll go to a Holiday Camp at Hayling Island, Hampshire," I said, showing him where Hayling Island was. "We'll see how it goes and what I can afford." I hugged him and he kissed my cheek.

I thought a lot about returning to Barbados, but I was not ready, nor did I have the courage, to face the shame and victimisation which would inevitably follow such a move. I couldn't bear to hear Wilfred say, "I told you so." I didn't dare write and tell Roy the truth either. No, better I kept the Barbados connections in the dark for the moment. I did write to Roy, however, telling him about my secretarial job at Battersea College and asking him to write to me there, giving him the excuse that I got the letters quicker. It was, of course, a little white lie but Roy wouldn't have known that.

It did not occur to me that Albert would have let anyone in Barbados know – except his parents, perhaps, but they would not go yapping their mouths off because of the shame which they would have to face. If Albert did write to them, he would probably have told them a mountain of lies anyhow.

I was busy typing away in the office one day in September 1959, when the phone rang and Nadine the copy typist called out to me, "For you, Samantha."

The male voice on the other end was strange but Barbadian. "Mrs Wetherby? This is Edson Kellman."

I frowned. "I'm sorry?"

"Edson Kellman. Kellman, your father's butler? I am his son."

Nadine jumped when I almost exploded into the phone. "Good God! Kellie's son, Edson! Where are you – in London?"

"Yes, ma'am." Yes *ma'am*?

"Please, Edson, not *ma'am*. Just Sam, or Samantha. My God, I can't believe it. What are you doing in London, and how did you find me?"

"Long story, Mrs … sorry, Samantha."

"I'm dying to talk to you, Edson. Could you come around to my flat this evening? I'm usually home by six." I gave him full directions how to get to the flat and rang off.

"An old friend?" Nadine asked me.

I laughed. "Not exactly. I don't even know the guy, but I know his father very well." I didn't dare tell her that 'the father' was my father's butler! I would have been branded immediately. Middle-class snob – and knowing Nadine, with her typical Cockney sense of humour, it would have been characteristic of her to reply, "Blimey, excuse *me*, Mrs Courtney of Curzon Street!"

Edson turned up at a quarter to seven. A slim, gangling, dark young man, with slightly bat ears, the usual moustache which is the trademark of black men, and a ready smile which showed all his teeth. Not really a handsome guy, but not ugly. He looked very smart in grey flannel pants, a white shirt, striped tie and a black blazer.

We went up to my first floor flat and I introduced him to Ray, who was watching a cartoon on television. He lifted Ray up, held him off to look at him, and said, "You're good-looking, just like your mother." Ray didn't quite know what to make of this so he squirmed and Edson put him down.

"Sit down, Edson. Cup of tea, coffee, or something stronger? Afraid I don't have any Barbados rum."

"You do now," said Edson, delving into a paper bag he had brought with him and digging out a bottle of Mount Gay rum. Best rum in the world! I was not fond of rum, but just to see Mount Gay again made me homesick but happy.

I took the bottle and thanked Edson, asking him if he wished a drink, but he said he would prefer a cup of coffee.

Ray had had his supper, and as soon as the cartoon had finished, I hustled him off to bed.

To show gratitude, I poured myself a small drink of rum, added some water, and Edson and I sat down to have a very long chat.

"So, tell me everything, Edson, and I mean *everything!*"

"Well, for a start, let me just say that my father is worried sick about you. You know he always seems to know what is going on, and he had heard that you and Albert had split up."

I was a little concerned about this. "How did he hear that, Edson?"

"You know my father goes to the rum shop every night to drink a beer. The shopkeeper told him that he had heard it from someone at the Wetherby farm." Edson sipped his coffee and continued.

"Dad contacted me, knowing I was shortly leaving for England to do engineering at Loughborough University." He paused and looked at me. "You do know that your father paid for my schooling at Harrison College, don't you?"

This was news to me, but then old Wilfred was full of surprises. "Edson, I did not even know your father was married and had a son!"

"Dad is not married to my mother, and my mother raised me, because as you know, my father was living and working with your family. But he helped to support my mother and me, and his name was put on my birth certificate. When I reached Harrison College age, someone seemed to think I was bright, my father told your father, and your father offered to pay the school fees."

I was having difficulty believing that Wilfred – the Wilfred I knew – would pay school fees at the top boys' school in Barbados for a black boy! On the other hand, I knew that my father cared a great deal for Kellman.

"Your father's not such a bad old stick, you know, Mrs … oh gosh … Samantha. I know all about your problems with him, and I know he is full of a lot of unnecessary prejudices, but he has been good to me and my father."

I nodded. "Glad to hear that, Edson, and to know that you have gained a place at a university to do engineering – congratulations. But – the sixty-four million dollar question – how did you find me at Battersea College?"

He smiled. "My father again. You know he cares a lot about you."

I was surprised by this submission. "*Kellie*? Cares about *me*?"

"That surprises you, I know, but it is true. He was always talking about you whenever he visited my mother and me. He said you were full of spunk and you had a social conscience. At one time, just before you left Barbados, he was very worried about you. He knew you were friendly with Albert and he had no use for Albert."

"Yes, but surely that was because of Albert's colour, and as he boldly told me, Albert was not my *class*."

"True. But more than that, he did not like Albert himself. He used to refer to him as that 'no-good bum', and when you left the island with Albert, he was afraid you would come to a sticky end."

"Which I did. Oh, boy, you can't imagine just how sticky, Edson."

"Was it that bad?"

I leaned back in my chair and gazed at him. "Edson, I really don't wish to divulge the details because I don't want anyone at home to know what I went through. But I'll tell you this – it was by the grace of God that I found myself a good lawyer whose advice saved me the terrible embarrassment of having my divorce details splashed all over the daily newspapers. It could have been a particularly nasty divorce had I gone ahead with adultery and cruelty, but my lawyer advised me to go for desertion on the grounds of mental cruelty. Albert was the guilty party and the Legal Aid system paid my lawyer. And by the way, I'm still waiting to hear how you found me."

"Oh, yes. Well, my father was so worried that he telephoned your friend, Roy, at the antique shop and told him that I was going to England and could he give him your new address. It seems you wrote and told your mother that you were moving and would send her your new address. My father asked your mother for the new address but she did not know it and suggested he try Roy. When my father spoke to Roy, he seemed concerned, told my dad that he had a 'sixth sense' that all was not well with you and he would be very happy if I would find out what's going on. He said you had written to say you could be contacted at Battersea College, where you were working."

"When are you actually entering Loughborough?"

"Next week. Why?"

"Edson, I do not wish people in Barbados to know the truth yet. I know that many of them will laugh their heads off at me and others will heap scorn on my head. 'Shame on her – serve her right', sort of thing. I can't face that right now."

"But my father ..."

"God bless old snooping Kellie! Write and tell him you've seen me and Ray, and we're just fine. Yes, you can say that Albert and I have split up – divorced and all that, but that I have a good job and a pleasant little flat, and leave it at that. Okay?"

"Can I reveal your address?"

"Sure. I'll write soon and give it to my mother, anyhow. She has softened up quite a bit towards me and she writes quite often, and sends things for Ray. In due course I will tell her the truth but not right now."

"Can I see you once more before I go to Loughborough, Sam?"

"Of course. Just call me at work and we'll arrange something."

Edson looked uncomfortable for a moment and shifted in his chair. "Uhm, my father gave me some money to take you to dinner if you would go with me."

What a right turn up for the books! Crafty old Kellie. Send Edson to butter her up to find out what the hell is going on in her life. I smiled.

"Edson, I would love that. Where are you staying?"

"In a small hotel in Bayswater. Your father booked it and paid for it."

"I should have known. Bajans who come over to London always stay in Bayswater!"

"Yes. Your father told me so. There are a lot of good little restaurants around that area, or we could go to Piccadilly, whatever is your choice."

We arranged that I would meet him on Saturday night at seven sharp at Queensway Tube Station and take it from there. I would have to arrange with the landlady, Mrs Mosham, to keep Ray for me. I had never asked her before, although she had offered many times. "You have no life of your own," she would fret. "You must get out some evenings and enjoy yourself. I will keep Ray for you."

That first evening, Edson and I talked well into the night until, fearful of missing a last bus, he left at ten thirty. He seemed to know his way around although he had only been in London for two weeks. He said he had not intended staying in London so long but circumstances had forced him to do so.

This was the London of the late 1950s, going into the sixties. Boatloads of West Indians were flocking to Britain every month. During the early fifties, when the first batches had started arriving, they were greeted with open arms. Accommodation and jobs were found for them easily. However, they were now descending on Britain in droves and resentment was building up. The British were fearful that their jobs and homes were in jeopardy, and the men felt they were losing their women to the 'horny' black men! Furthermore, the British noticed with distaste that the habits and standards of most of the immigrants were not in keeping with their own. *"They spit in the streets,"* they said; *"They pee at the side of the road, in public,"* (Hello! So do the Frogs!) *"Their houses are filthy* and overcrowded," "They're loud and raucous," "Their foul language is unacceptable," "They're just **different**."

Signs appeared on front doors of houses, declaring: 'FLAT FOR RENT. NO COLOUREDS.' I got a good giggle out of that. First, the British invite them to come over from the Caribbean and welcome them with open arms, then they do a complete about-turn. The soap box orators at Speaker's Corner in Hyde Park did a number. *"Go back to the West Indies, you blacks, we don't want you here!"* No doubt followers of Sir Oswald Moseley and Enoch Powell. Moseley's anti-Semitic views were well known, and now he was starting on the blacks. Before the blacks, it had been the Irish who had suffered similar insults. But at least the Irish could not be identified unless they spoke.

For the first time in a couple of years I felt really happy. I actually felt as if Edson were a family member from home, and I became quite excited when I thought about Saturday night. Mrs Mosham readily agreed to have Ray. "Do you good to get out for a change," she said.

Bang on time Saturday evening, I arrived at Queensway Underground Station to find Edson there waiting for me.

"So, what's it to be – local, or Piccadilly?" he asked, but did not give me a chance to reply. "I suggest we go to Piccadilly. There's a Chinese restaurant there that I like. You like Chinese food?"

"Love it."

We went to the Chinese restaurant in Piccadilly.

I love the excitement of Piccadilly – all those hundreds of people milling around, some sitting on the steps of the Eros statue, lovers linking arms and strolling, others window-shopping, and some heading for cinemas or restaurants, just as Edson and I were.

I waded through the enormous menu and ordered something that was reasonably priced.

When Albert and I had first come over to London, I had hustled him over to Piccadilly where we had had a meal, also in a Chinese restaurant, and then we had walked to Trafalgar Square. We were such lovers in those days. What the hell had gone wrong? Looking back, I realised that nothing had ever been *right*. Only I was too blind to see it.

Edson ordered two glasses of wine. Just as I raised my glass in a toast, I glanced across the room and saw two men moving towards a table not far from ours. I replaced the glass on the table quickly and must have turned pale as I stared. My heart did a couple of flips – what my father would have called 'tachycardia', and Edson glanced over in the direction of my gaze.

"Is something wrong?" he asked.

It took me a while to answer. "I ... I know one of those guys who just sat at that table over there," I said, pointing with my chin. "His name is Tony Brownfield and he is from Barbados."

Edson looked at me hard. "Does that bother you – him being a white Bajan, seeing you with me?" He sounded hurt.

"Hell, no, Edson! Nothing like that. It's just that he and I were sort of going together before I ... well, made the mistake of my life." As I said these words, Tony, who was facing our table, glanced over and our eyes met and locked. His face slowly turned dark pink and I've no doubt mine did the opposite for I felt the blood draining from it. I realised I would have to make the first move, if I had read Tony's expression right. I did not recognise the other man with him but he was dressed like an Englishman.

I don't know how I got through the first course and I am sure Edson must have felt very uncomfortable, and that was the last thing I wanted, he being so kind to me and bringing a little joy into my life. However, the situation *vis-a-vis* colour and class had changed very little in Barbados, and although I had been married to a coloured man, Albert had been very clear-skinned in comparison to Edson. Edson would have grown up with prejudice all around him and he would have encountered it, in no uncertain terms, at Harrison College.

I chose strawberries and cream for dessert and when it was finished, I said to Edson, "Do you mind if I go over and say hello to Tony?" He did not mind.

"Tony Brownfield," I said, as I reached his table. "Well, well, well." Tony jumped up – always the gentleman – and so did the other man.

Tony said, "John, I'd like you to meet an old friend, Samantha ... er ..."

"Wetherby," I said clearly.

John and I shook hands and so did Tony and I. Long ago and far away he would have given me a kiss.

"Would you care to sit with us?" Tony said, looking across at Edson's table.

"I'd love to but I think not. My companion is Edson Kellman. You remember my father's butler, Kellie? Edson is his son and he is entering Loughborough College next week to do engineering."

Tony nodded. The expression on his face was difficult to read but he looked distinctly unhappy and uncomfortable. There was a slight frown on his face and his speech was cool, if nothing else. I thought it best to do all the talking.

"So what brings you over to London, Tony, and how is Greta?"

Tony shifted uncomfortably. "I'm in London on business. You probably don't know but I finished university in Canada, and went back to Barbados to work with my father. John is with the London firm associated with our business." He ignored my reference to Greta.

"Are you staying long in London?"

"I've been here one week already. Flew over from New York, where I did some more business for the firm, and I'm not sure exactly how long I'll be here, but probably for another few days."

"Where are you staying?"

"At the Regent Hotel – just around the corner from here."

What a juxtaposition – here, in one corner, is the rich white man from Barbados, entertaining his equally rich English friend, and here, in the other corner, is the poor 'white' Cinderella, and no doubt 'outcast', with her poor black friend from Barbados!

As Tony made no attempt whatsoever to enquire as to my situation, address, phone number or anything, I said lamely, "I'd better get back to my table. It was wonderful seeing you again, Tony, and nice meeting you, John."

As to what transpired between the two of them after I returned to my table, I can only hazard a guess. Tony would have filled John in with all my shocking details, only he would not have known my present situation and he would have wondered why I was out with another man instead of being at home with my husband.

God, he must have thought the worst of me! And there was nothing I could do about it.

As I lay in bed that night I thought a lot about Tony. It hurt terribly that I had not been able to enlighten him; not, I realised, that he had wanted to be enlightened. All his expressions had made that clear.

Edson phoned me before he left for Loughborough. "Thanks for being such good company the other evening. Thanks also for not bolting through the door before your friend, Tony, could see you with me."

"Edson, *please*. You must know damn well that I'm not like that. If no one else, your father would have told you that. He would never have asked you to look me up if he thought I would have snubbed you. You're a great guy and I want you to keep in touch, and any time you're in London again, please call me. Good luck and God bless."

13

Ray's first day at school was tearful for both of us. He clung to me and wanted to go back home. I managed to persuade him that he would have an exciting day, reluctantly left him, went into the office and had a good cry. Nadine was very understanding although she herself was not married and had no children.

However, Ray settled down quickly and began to enjoy school. During the school holidays, I found a lady, recommended by the Children's Welfare Department as a child minder, with whom I left him when I was at work.

At Christmas time, Ray and I drove through Oxford Street to see all the lights on Selfridges and all the other shops along the way, stretching across the road from shop to shop. Ray was ecstatic. He had seen them before but now he was at a more impressionable age and they meant more to him.

I had hoped that Edson could make it down to London for Christmas, but he said he couldn't afford it so he would be spending Christmas in his tiny lodgings in Leicester.

We got the usual Christmas card from Les in Cornwall, and in it he wrote, *'No excuses next year – come to Cornwall to visit!'* And I thought, I might just take you up on that, Leslie Simons.

Which I did. I got three weeks' vacation in August and I packed up, slung the suitcases in the trunk of the car, and Ray and I set off – at seven o'clock in the morning to beat the traffic – for St Ives, hoping too that the little Morris Minor would take us that distance.

Knowing that it would be too tiring to attempt the entire journey in one day, and also, admitting to a desire to recapture some of my youth and school days, I decided to overnight in Bournemouth and, yes, I wanted to pamper myself a bit. So only the best would do. Nothing less than the Highcliffe Hotel – perched on the cliffs, where Wilfred and Ellen had always stayed during their visits to Bournemouth.

We drove past my old school and I pointed it out to Ray. He was not impressed. He just asked if there was a swimming pool, which of course there wasn't.

We drove on into Bournemouth, parked the car and had lunch in the restaurant at Bobby's department store before checking into the hotel.

It was crammed jam full of a lot of rich old gits, some in bath chairs, others walking around with straight backs and heads in the air. Ex-Cheltenham Ladies College, Roedean and maybe a few good old Etonians – who knew? I got a lot of joy out of watching them. Ray did not. He complained that we were staying in an old peoples' home! Not one young child in sight.

We set out immediately after an early room-service breakfast next morning, reaching St. Ives around lunchtime. God, I thought, I've never seen so many steep hills in all my life. Nor so many seagulls – they were everywhere, whirling and screeching. Ray was fascinated.

We had some lunch in a little cafe on the waterfront and then set off to find Jean's parents' greengrocer's shop.

Les spotted us on the pavement and rushed out to greet us. He hugged both of us and ushered us into the little office at the back where Jean's mum, Mrs Bowling, greeted us warmly and put the kettle on for a welcome cuppa. She gave Ray a glass of fresh orange juice. She was delighted to see him again and couldn't get over how he had grown.

"Dad's at home," she said, referring to Mr Bowling. "His arthritis is kicking up. Les will take you over to the house after a cup of tea. What about some lunch?"

"We've had some, thanks."

We chatted non-stop but Ray was becoming restless so we drove over to the house with Les giving directions. It was up an unbelievably steep, narrow hill, and at the back of the house, steep steps led up the hill to a terraced garden.

Mr Bowling greeted us at the front door and limped his way back into the living room while Les took Ray and me up to the spare bedroom. Les took me out to dinner that night while Ray stayed with the Bowlings. If St Ives was beautiful in the day, it was even more beautiful at night with the lights along the bay and in the quaint little shops and restaurants.

I slept like a log that night, even though the seagulls kept up their relentless squawking and mewing. To me, it was a delightful sound. To the Bowlings it was a God-awful racket and they said they felt like shooting the bloody birds!

We all had a huge breakfast next morning with bacon, eggs, sausages and fried tomatoes, and I felt very spoiled.

Les said to me, "The weather forecast is good – sunny and warm, they say. Mum says she will entertain Ray while Dad runs the shop and, if you would like, you and I can go over to Land's End. I have a beat-up old Triumph Herald which we could use, and give yours a rest after that long journey. How does that sound?"

"Sounds fine to me." I asked Ray if he would mind staying with Mrs. Bowling and he seemed excited. She had promised to take him down on the bay where all the fishing boats were, and for ice cream and a ride on a donkey.

Land's End was picturesque and somewhat romantic. It reminded me of North Point in Barbados with rugged cliffs and a wild, turbulent sea far below. When you stood on the cliffs at North Point, you could imagine solid, reliable old England four thousand miles off to the North East, and when you stood on the cliffs at Land's End, you could picture beautiful Barbados glowing in the Caribbean sun, way off to the South West. Tears came to my eyes as I gazed off to the South West.

Les and I sat on the grass-covered rocks and watched the sea birds. We could just make out the Isles of Scilly in the distance.

"Are you happy here in Cornwall, Les?"

"Pretty much so, Sam. I miss London at times and, as you know, I get up there very seldom. The shop keeps me pretty busy and Dad is getting down now, you know. Mum and I do most of the work, and we have persuaded him to take it easy."

"What about your own parents?"

"My mum. My dad died and my mum lives in Whitby, Yorkshire. She married again but I don't particularly like the man, so I don't get up there often. In fact, I haven't been up to Whitby since Jeanie died." Here, he paused and looked at me. "God, Sam, I miss her like hell."

I grabbed his hand. "So do I, Les. So do I." We both shed some tears and were silent for some time, each wrapped up in our memories of Jean.

Les was the first to break the silence. He picked up a small stick and fiddled with it. "Sam, I don't know how you will take what I am going to say, but it must be said." He cleared his throat. "Just before Jean died, she … she made me promise her something. She said that when your divorce was final, and if ever I wanted to get married again ... oh, God, this is difficult." He looked away, and it was an embarrassing moment because there was nothing I could say although I pretty well knew what was to follow. Then he swiftly said, without further hesitation, "She said I should marry you."

I looked into his flushed, chubby face – Les was not a tall man, he was stout but not fat, with round, pleasant features, and he wore glasses.

I watched a seagull land close to us. We had been eating Cornish pasties which Les had bought, and the bird wanted some. It was not in the least bit shy and it came right up to me when I held out my hand with some crumbs.

Les made a motion as if to chase it away. "Bloody buggers nip pretty hard, you know." But the bird had already forced its beak between my fingers and picked off the crumbs.

"Aggressive birds, those," said Les.

"I love birds, Les. It did not peck me."

Les shifted his position so that he could look directly at me. "You did not comment on what I said. What is your answer?"

I laughed. "Les, as far as I know, you made a statement, not asked a question!"

"You're right, Sam. Now I shall ask the question. Would you consider marrying me? You know I would welcome Ray and love him as my own son. The son I never had."

I sighed. "Leslie, you have knocked the ground from under my feet and right now I can't think straight. I appreciate your offer and love you for it. But I simply can't give a cut and dried answer to such a question. To begin with, you have admitted it was *Jean's* wish. Do you really think marriage between us would last on such a foundation?"

Les reached for my hand. "Oh gosh, that was clumsy of me. Look, Sam, I admit it was Jean's wish but I have kept in touch with you and Ray since living in Cornwall. Doesn't that tell you something? I loved Jean with all my heart and I love the memory of her, but there are all kinds of love. I can't say I am passionately in love with you but I care for you a lot, and in fact it amounts to love of a sort. It would grow – I know that for sure. I haven't even looked at another woman since Jean died – that's the God's truth. But I have thought a lot about you, and Ray. And what's more, you deserve a decent life, Sam. You and Ray." He looked away shyly when he said this.

I looked away and was silent for a while. Then I squeezed Les's hand. "God bless you, Leslie Simons. You have given me back my self respect and self confidence. Do you know how dirty I felt after all I went through with Albert and that girl Sheila? For a long time I did not even want to see another man. Then the son of my father's butler came over to England to do engineering, and he contacted me. He's a few years younger than me, and …"

"Oh God, I'm too late," Les said, holding his head.

"Would you please let me finish? This guy is a student. His father gave him money to take me out to dinner before he went to Leicester. His father is worried about me and begged Edson to make sure I was okay. That's literally all there is to it, okay? He is not my type, and come to think of it, I don't even know who is my type any longer!"

"I'm sorry, Sam. I shouldn't have misjudged you. I've just been bloody clumsy all round." He stood up quickly and brushed the grass from his trousers. "We should be getting back now, I suppose."

"Les, we can't leave it like this. I have to explain some things. First of all, foremost in my mind is going back to Barbados to live. Not just yet, of course, but maybe in a year or two. I have to psyche up myself to face that situation first.

"Secondly, I am not in love with you, and I don't know that I could make you happy. I am fond of you as a friend and I hope that never changes. I am truly flattered by your proposal but it would take a hell of a lot of soul-searching on my part. Can you understand that?"

He nodded. "That's reasonable enough. Sam, have you completely got over Albert?"

I laughed. "Ages ago. I went through the hurt stage and then the hate stage, and then there was – nothing. No feeling whatsoever – no love, no hate. I was suddenly at peace with myself. I have let go entirely. It's past history. I don't even think Ray misses him. He never asks for his father."

Les looked thoughtful. "Just as well, I suppose."

I told Les I would not dismiss his proposal from my mind by any means but it would require lots of careful thought.

We drove back to St Ives, both of us in pensive moods.

The weather held good except for one day during our stay in St Ives. We even swam in the sea on one particularly hot day. Les drove Ray and me all over the place, sometimes in my car, sometimes in his. We went to Bodmin Moor and had lunch at the Jamaica Inn, and we drove north as far as Newquay.

Les took me out to dinner a couple of times, and one day the Bowlings shut up the shop for a couple of hours and I treated them all to lunch.

I felt as if I were in a different world, a different time zone where everything was all play and no work. The Bowlings and Les certainly pampered Ray and me. I could not always understand Mr Bowling because he spoke with a broad Cornish accent – although I should by rights have understood him because they say that the Barbadian accent is similar to the English West Country accent.

Our week seemed to whirl by but, alas, it was time to pack up and head for London. Les took me out to dinner on the last night and once again he repeated his proposal and once again I begged him to give me time to think it over. It was a tempting proposition while I was in this idyllic environment but I had to face reality back in London.

The drive back to London took just over seven hours. We had left St Ives at seven in the morning, stopping in Launceston for petrol and a light breakfast, and then again at Salisbury for lunch. Ray slept most of the way and I was tempted to stop again and call it a day but the thought of having to spend more money for a hotel room was not to my liking so I plodded along, finally reaching Wandsworth Common just before three o'clock.

There were a couple of letters lying on the hall table. They had been received at the office and Nadine had kindly slipped them through the letterbox. Mrs Mosham had placed them on the table to await my return. One was from Roy and the other from Ellen. There was also one from Edson, addressed directly to the flat.

I fixed Ray and myself something to eat and drink. He was as fresh as a daisy because he had had plenty of sleep in the car. He went straight to the living room and turned on the television to watch his favourite cartoon. I went to the bedroom to read the letters and have a bit of a kip.

Edson's letter was short, just a few lines to ask how I had enjoyed Cornwall and if everything was okay, and to let me know that once again, his father was very concerned over me because numerous rumours were reaching Barbados and he, Edson, certainly hadn't started them.

My mother did not beat about the bush in her letter either. She demanded to know what was happening to me. She said that she had noticed for some time that Kellman was not his usual self; something was bothering him. So she cornered him one day and he broke down and admitted to her that he was worried about me.

"He is like a family member and he cares for you and Gwennie, as he cares for your father and I, and he gets worried if he thinks something is wrong ..." she wrote, *"... he told me emphatically that he thought you should never have married 'that scamp', and although Edson has seen you and assured him that you are okay, he still feels that Edson is holding back something.*

Sam, we all make mistakes in life – none of us is infallible – and if your marriage has been a mistake, learn from it and move on."

She went on to say that the very fact that I had asked Roy to send letters to Battersea College tells them all something, and would I please enlighten them, as they all stood ready to help me if necessary. *"Believe it or not, your father asked me to tell you that."*

Good old Ellen. Wilfred? Well, I wasn't so sure. He would be willing to help, yes, but there would be strings attached. *"Come home and help me test blood and pee"*, sort of thing.

As to Roy's letter, it made me hoot with laughter which was the anticlimax I needed after reading Ellen's letter. Why was I working in a staid office near Battersea Dogs' Home when I could have had a stall down the Portobello Market selling antiques? Why move from Southfields (close enough to Middle-Class Wimbledon) and go to Wandsworth Common to live among working class Cockneys? And was I living on Kit-e-Kat, as it was alleged that 'Wogs' were doing in Britain? If so, he could send me some Puss 'n' Boots – far superior. Good old Roy – he hadn't changed! He ended off the letter by begging me to write to Ellen and put her in the picture.

His reference to the Portobello Market saddened me. Jean and I often used to trundle down there searching for bargains, and I once bought a lovely little copper kettle which Roy would have envied. Only paid five quid for it.

Ray was shaking me and calling, "Mummy, Mummy, the door bell!" I jumped up and looked at my watch. It was just after six o'clock. I had slept for two hours.

I groggily went downstairs and opened the door wondering who it could be. It was Albert. He looked thin and a bit haggard. He held out a small package to Ray, who was beside me in the hallway. "Belated birthday present, son," he said.

I invited him upstairs to the living room. I couldn't stop yawning. I would probably have slept another hour.

"Edson Kellman got you tired out?" This from Albert. It took me by complete surprise and I could only stare at him. My tired brain was befuddled.

"Think because this is a big country news don't get around?" he asked me.

Ray had unwrapped his gift. It was one of those wind-up helicopters. I suggested that he take it into his bedroom to try it out and when he got it working he could return to the living room. I did not wish him to witness a confrontation between his father and I. When he had gone, I turned to Albert. "I don't know what filth you have in your mind which appears to be perpetually in a sewer, but I have absolutely no explanation for you. I owe you *nothing*, so if you've nothing else to say ..."

"Oh, I have. It seems I was not black enough for you!"

I stared at this virtual stranger before me. I couldn't believe what I was hearing. Had he gone mad? Quickly I told myself that I must not lose my cool, no matter what. The man was trying to raise my hackles. As if he hadn't done me enough harm, two years after our divorce here he is again, trying to harass me.

I opened the living room door intending to usher him out but he grabbed my arm, spun me around and tried to kiss me. I was so utterly disgusted that I raised my leg and kneed him in the testicles. He bent over double and I ran downstairs and shouted for Mrs Mosham. She came out of her door quickly. "What's wrong, love?"

"Mrs Mosham, please call the police."

But just then, Albert came downstairs, one hand grabbing his crotch, and without a backward glance went out of the front door.

Mrs Mosham shook her head from side to side. "Queer one, 'im. What did he do?"

"The bastard tried to kiss me in a very aggressive manner. I know he is Ray's father, Mrs Mosham, but I want you to promise me that if ever he comes here and I am out, don't let him in, okay?

"Wouldn't dream of it. Not after what you told me he done to you and that darling little boy. Sorry to say it, Samantha, but I don't have much use for them darkies. Scare me, they do."

"They're not all bad, Mrs Mosham. Take it from me – I grew up among black people in Barbados, you know. I just happened to pick the wrong one!"

Ray had heard the commotion and came downstairs with his helicopter. "Where's Daddy?"

"He left, honey. Had an urgent appointment. Said to say goodbye to you." I kissed him on his head.

I thought over the incident as I lay in bed that night. What was Albert up to? Would I be forced to look for new accommodation and hide from him? I couldn't do that because of the Court ruling giving him visiting rights. But what if I went to live in Cornwall? Of course, I would only do that out of desperation and that would be very unfair to Les. I put it out of my mind, turned over and went to sleep.

14

A T the end of 1962, my boss, the kindly old Austrian professor
of chemistry, retired, and in his place came a short-tempered
Englishman whose rather hard right-wing views I despised. He
was always going on about 'the Wogs invading Britain' and he was
no lover of Jews either.

I got chatting with the Librarian in the College cafeteria one day
and she said her secretary was leaving to get married and if I would
like the position all I had to do was put in for a transfer, which I
did. Nadine also asked to be transferred to another department
and we met up sometimes in the cafeteria.

I became well and truly ensconced in the Library, having got the
transfer, and loved being surrounded by books of every description.

Ray was doing very well at school. He was tall for his age and had
lost all his baby fat. He was crazy about cricket. He was, after all, a
West Indian!

Albert had not been to visit since that last dreadful incident and I
was not sorry. Edson came down to London a couple of times and we
visited the West Indian Students' Centre in Earls Court to drink a
couple of corn 'n' oils (rum and falernum) in the bar and to exchange
news and views of the Caribbean with other West Indian students. I
told Edson about the incident with Albert and he was shocked. "I
think that guy has a few screws loose," he remarked.

I had stalled Les for two years and was still no nearer to a
decision. I was finding it hard to make two ends meet but I had no
intention of marrying a man just for security. Les was too nice a
guy to take advantage of. Strangely enough, he didn't see it that
way. He was very fond of Ray and me and, in fact, the previous
year he took a few days off from the shop and came up to London
to visit us. He stayed at a bed & breakfast in Streatham, although I
had offered him Ray's room and Ray could have slept with me. He
did not wish to embarrass me, he said.

I knew I would have to make a decision soon, I couldn't keep
him dangling at the end of a rope forever.

I wrote to Ellen soon after I received Roy's letter:

Dear Mum,

I know you are concerned about me so I will explain everything as briefly as possible. I hate writing about unfortunate things in detail.

Albert and I have been divorced since January 1958. Things did not work out between us, and they deteriorated to the point where I thought it best to call it quits. He had a girlfriend in Barbados before he and I got together and she was pregnant for him before he left for England. She came over to England with her baby daughter and contacted him, and that's the story in a nutshell. (I'm sure Kellie filled you in on that!) We sold the house, because it was part of the divorce agreement, and I have this little flat at Wandsworth Common. I got full custody of Ray, and he and I are doing just fine. He is bright and doing well at school.

I have been transferred from the Chemistry Department to the Library at the College and am enjoying my work. Please do not worry about me, Mum. Everything is fine.

I have some very nice friends living in St Ives and Ray and I recently spent a week with them. St Ives is everything it is cracked up to be – just beautiful. We shall probably go again next year if I can afford it.

I have written to Gwennie a couple of times but she has not replied. How are they all doing Down Under? Say hello to Kellie for me and tell him I appreciate his sending Edson to make sure I'm OK. Give Meg a big hug for me and tell her I miss her and her cooking!

Love to you and Dad,
Sam

That letter must have done the trick, because Ellen and I traded letters quite frequently after that, and she always ended off by saying that Wilfred sent his love and assurances that if Ray and I wished to come home, we only had to say so. Only I was not ready to go home yet. It was no longer a case of fearing the repercussions of such a move, for now that the ice was broken it was not such a threat. Rather I was thinking of Ray's education, and upbringing. Where would he stand in Barbadian society, knowing his background? Would he turn out to be a complete snob, like his grandfather, and ignore his father's side of the family? Or would he take the opposite route? If he came under Wilfred's influence, God help him!

It all boiled down to the fact that as he grew older and gained more understanding of the world around him, I would have to steer him in a middle course, and God knows, I was not much good at steering my own course, let alone that of my son.

If I took Les up on his offer, it would be extremely difficult to steer Ray in a middle course. There were few, if any, coloured people in St Ives. He would grow up among all white English boys. I would prefer he were in a mixed society. The whole thing would call for very serious thought. It was far from cut and dried.

Britain was reeling under the onslaught, not only of West Indian immigrants, but also of Indians from India, and Pakistanis – most of whom were Muslims. Different cultures, different beliefs. The soapbox orators at Speaker's Corner in Hyde Park were doing a number. It was great fun to go and listen to them. Once, a man standing next to me, thinking me to be English, murmured, "He's dead right, you know, all these bloody wogs crawling all over Britain, turning the place into a slum!" I remained non-committal. It was at times such as these that I missed Jean. She and I would have had a good giggle together.

Ray was showing a great deal of interest in history so I decided to take him to the Tower of London. He knew the story of the two princes locked in the tower and he was fascinated. I had embarked on a programme of visiting as many of the historical sights around London as we could because Ray was now eight, and if we were going to return to Barbados to enable him to enter Harrison College in another two years' time, he would need to be well primed to sit the entrance examination.

Ray grabbed my arm when he noticed a black lady with, pre-sumably, her son, over by the cannons at the Tower. I had taught him never to point at people so he nodded his head in their direction and said excitedly, "Mum, that wog goes to my school!"

I jumped. Then I stood stock-still and stared at Ray. "That *what*?"

Ray must have sensed strong emotions in me because he mumbled, "That – boy – with his mum – I think he goes to my school."

I pulled Ray over to a bench away from the mum and son and motioned him to sit down.

"Ray, did I hear you refer to that boy as a 'wog'?"

Ray shook his head. I think he was a bit scared because of my initial reaction.

"Who taught you that word?" Stupid question really, because the word was used freely all over Britain.

"Kids at school, Mum. They call all dark people wogs."

"They're ignorant, son, and you must never ever do it, okay? You, me, your dad – we're all of mixed race so maybe they could call us wogs too. You wouldn't like that, would you?" He shook his head.

"The term 'wog', I believe, originated in the days of the Indian Raj. When Britain ruled India. The British, with their usual diplomacy, when referring to a dark skinned Indian, would use the term western oriental gentleman – w.o.g. The term became general and now it applies to all coloured peoples – Indians, Pakistanis, Africans, West Indians, and it is used in an insulting way."

Ray was silent and thoughtful. He appeared to understand. But did he really? Race, as a topic, had never really been discussed in our family. There had been no need. Ray had become accustomed to our frequent black visitors, just as he had known Jean and Les and other white friends.

"Do you wish to go over and say hello to the boy?" I asked Ray. He shook his head. "He doesn't play with me at school and he fights a lot." Different ball game. Poor boy would probably end up fighting his way through life in England, no matter what.

I had recently installed a telephone, due to pressure from Les, Roy and Ellen. Ellen in particular. "How can we know how you are all the time when letters take almost a week?" She had sent a bank draft which she said Wilfred insisted should pay for the installation of a telephone. It helped with a few of my bills as well.

The phone rang just as I was preparing supper for Ray and myself one Saturday evening. It was Roy. "Hello, duckie! What are you doing? It's one thirty p.m. here and I've just finished stuffing my guts with flying fish and cou-cou. Absolutely delicious."

"Roy! Wonderful to hear you. As a matter of fact, I was just preparing some supper – baked beans on toast and a salad."

"Bet you wish it were flying fish and cou-cou though. Wish I could send you some. Sam, I'll be as brief as possible. Actually, a letter is on the way telling you everything, but I couldn't wait to tell you – Guy and I are relocating to Martinique. We're closing down the shop here next month. Found a heavenly spot in Fort-de-France and the antique business there is more lucrative than in Barbados. Given you all the details in my letter. Wish us luck!"

"Oh, Roy, I'm so happy for you, and I hope you and Guy will do well. For my part, I am sad. I mentioned in a letter, if you remember, that I am seriously considering returning to Barbados so that Ray can enter Harrison College and get a good education. That won't be for another two years or so, but you'll be gone and I will miss you."

"Don't worry, ducks, when you come home and are settled in, I will send an airline ticket for you to visit Martinique. Everything okay with you? Thanks for your letter with the sketchy details of your divorce and everything. Sorry it didn't work out, Sam, but glad you and Ray came out unscathed, and at least you have him."

"Roy, before you buzz off to Martinique, please find out the Harrison College requirements for entrance, will you?"

"As good as done. Give that darling boy a hug for me. Will call you again before we leave. Keep well."

I stood by the phone for a while after we had both rung off. I was more upset by Roy's decision than I had let on. I had hoped to walk into my old job when we reached Barbados, to save Wilfred's inevitable intervention.

Ever since I had seen Tony at the Chinese restaurant in Piccadilly, I had thought about him a lot. Other than Albert, he was the only man I had come close to being in love with. Had I not been so blindly and foolishly in love with Albert, perhaps I would now be Mrs Tony Brownfield. Had he married Greta on the rebound? It didn't seem likely – Tony was too stable a person for that. There had to have been some chemistry between them, although I could just imagine Greta stirring up a witch's brew of love potions to 'fix' Tony with! Well, whatever, I had lost him for good so there was no point in thinking of him. I couldn't forget how handsome he had looked at the Chinese restaurant, and his face appeared before me in my thoughts and dreams far too regularly for my liking.

I don't know if it was because of thoughts of Tony running around in my head but suddenly I began to think more of Les and his proposal, which, as far as I knew, still held good. Dared I reconsider, and think seriously about going to St Ives? If I could pick up a decent job there, I could still take Ray to Barbados and enter him into Harrison College, come back to England and send for him during the long summer vacation. But that would mean he would have to stay with Ellen and Wilfred during the other holiday periods. In fact, he would have to live with them.

Back to square one – he would be under Wilfred's influence. I was well and truly wedged between a rock and a hard place and I needed to consult someone for advice and suggestions. But who? If I were in Barbados, I would immediately think of Roy, but to write all my concerns in a letter would be too taxing. Besides which, Roy was busy getting ready to relocate to Martinique.

Again, as fate had intervened once before in my life at a turning point, it intervened again, in the form of a long letter from both Ellen and Wilfred. For some time, Wilfred had been considering joining Gwennie and Richard and their two children in Australia. A few white Barbadians had already packed up and gone to live in Australia and New Zealand, and some had gone to Canada. Wilfred said, in his portion of a joint letter, *"Did I not tell you that this would happen one day? Did I not predict that the blacks would one day take over in Barbados and that life would be hell for white people? Well, they are now behaving as if they were the first to inhabit the island. They say it is their island and the whites should leave. Grantley Adams' party was voted out and we now have the Democratic Labour Party, led by a Mr Errol Barrow. He is a man that I have a great deal of respect for in many ways, but he is a politician, and because of how feelings are running right now, he has to kowtow to the blacks. Barbados is finished, take it from me."*

The good news in the letter – if it could be called good news – was that they would leave Barbados on a Dutch passenger ship and spend a week or two in London before boarding a P & O liner from Southampton to Sydney.

Time simply flew until that day in October 1963 when Ray and I went to Waterloo Station to meet the boat train from Southampton. Wilfred and Ellen had aged, naturally, but they both looked well. They were very impressed with Ray, who was a polite, well-mannered child. He stretched out his hand in greeting but Ellen would have none of that – she hugged him and kissed him. Wilfred shook his hand and patted his head. "Fine-looking young man you've got here, Sam," he said. I was amazed!

They gave me the name of their hotel in Bayswater, climbed into a taxi with loads of luggage, and Ray and I walked to my car over in the car park and drove to their hotel.

Two weeks later, we were all back at Waterloo. Wilfred and Ellen were travelling on the *Bournemouth Belle* to Southampton. They had enjoyed their two weeks in London although the days were chilly and the nights were cold, and Wilfred hated cold weather. They had visited my flat a few times and I had taken them driving in the old Morris Minor that was holding together, but only just.

On their last night at the hotel, Wilfred had launched into one of his little pep talks to me. "Sam, I know how stubborn – you call it *independent* – you can be, but I want you to know that we have rented out Ginger Lily to an American couple for two years. They would have taken it for longer but I had you in mind. I know you wish to return to Barbados, and the house is yours – rent-free – for as long as you like. Please don't do your independent stunt on me, just be practical. You will need somewhere to live and it will be good for young Ray to be on the beach."

I nodded because there were tears in my eyes and I was too choked up to talk. I felt like saying to him, "You old sod, don't you see what has brought us closer together? A coloured man!" Which was true. Had it not been due to my marriage to Albert and all I had been through, that my father and I had softened up towards each other? He still wanted to rule my life to a certain extent – paying for my telephone, and now offering me free accommodation in Barbados – but somehow I did not feel such resentment. Instead I felt gratitude.

When the *Bournemouth Belle* pulled out of Waterloo Station, I broke down and sobbed. My darling little Ray put his arms around me and said, "Don't cry, Mum, you'll see Granny and Grandpa again."

15

A whole year had gone by and we had not been anywhere on vacation. I would have to remedy that this year. It was true that during Ray's summer holidays, when I also took my annual three weeks, we had driven all over the place – as far south as Eastbourne, and as far north as Stratford-on-Avon; as far east as Southend and Shoeburyness. We had taken boat rides on the Thames and we had visited Windsor Castle and Hampton Court Palace. I wanted Ray to get the true feeling and meaning of Great Britain, its pageantry and tradition, and, hopefully, to love it as I did.

I telephoned Les. "Can we come and visit this summer?"

He was thrilled. "About bloody time! In August?"

"Yes. We'll travel by train though, as the old car is getting down a bit and I wouldn't want to risk her on such a long journey."

"Tell you what then, come to Plymouth and I'll meet you there in my car. Just give me a buzz when you know the date and I'll be there."

"Are you sure? Plymouth is quite a distance from St Ives."

"You let me worry about that. Just be there! Talk to you again before then."

Ray was ten years old. He was a tall lad for his age, and most people thought he was twelve. His features were a mixture of Albert's and mine. He had Albert's liquid brown eyes and forehead, a short mouth but fullish lips, and my nose and chin. His hair was soft, brown and wavy. His interest in history had deepened and he was very much into cricket, tennis and football. He was also keen to learn horse-riding, as he knew I had done so many years ago at New Milton in the New Forest. When Wilfred had learned of this, he sent some money so that I could pay riding school fees and I took Ray to a riding school in nearby Streatham. I had not wanted to accept money from Wilfred on a regular basis – through false pride, I suppose – but at Christmas time when he had sent one hundred pounds for Ray and me, and after I had bought Ray some stuff, I went on the rampage at a Harrods January sale after Christmas and bought myself a classy outfit costing thirty quid.

It was a warm day in August when Ray and I boarded the train at Paddington and arrived in Plymouth just after mid-afternoon. Les hugged us and we all bundled into his car – he now had a Sunbeam Rapier – and headed for St Ives. By six o'-clock we were all sitting in the Bowlings' living room having supper and chatting away nineteen to the dozen. There was a lot of news to catch up on.

Two days later, Les and I took a ride out to Land's End and I unburdened my concerns and problems; we discussed everything in detail. I took Les's hand in mine and said, "Les, you have been so good to me and Ray and I love you for it, but I don't know if it is enough. I mean enough for marriage. I am surprised you haven't found someone nice after all these years; someone you could love and settle down with. You can't spend the rest of your life living with the Bowlings, as nice as they are, surely?"

"I wanted to leave and find a little flat for myself but they would have none of it. I don't wish to be ungracious to them – hell, they love me like a son. I can't leave them unless you and I got married. They would settle for that as we have talked it over. They like you a lot and they love Ray, as you know."

"How about if I take Ray to Barbados, see him settled into Harrison College and then come back to you?"

Les looked at me quickly. "You mean it?"

I nodded.

"But where would he live, now that your parents have gone to Australia?"

"With Kellman. Wilfred bought him a little cottage near the sea in Christ Church with half an acre of land attached so that he could keep livestock and have a kitchen garden."

Les was quiet for a while. Then he said, somewhat reluctantly, "What about standards of upbringing and that sort of thing – wasn't Kellman your family butler?"

I laughed. "Kellman is as much a snob as my father is, Les. He would be very strict with Ray and censor his social activities. He would make sure that Ray did not mix with bad company."

"Have you talked to Ray about this?"

"Not yet. I hadn't given it that much thought until now, be-cause I wanted to run it by you first. My parents' move to Australia did disrupt my plans considerably, but when my mother told me all about Kellie's new home and everything, the idea of Ray staying with him seemed pretty good. Ray could come over to England during the long summer holidays, and maybe – just *maybe* – if I pick up a decent job in St Ives, I could get over to Barbados occasionally."

Les nodded. "It sounds good in theory but you know it all hinges on how Ray would feel about it, don't you think? I mean, does it have to be Harrison College, Barbados, or could we send him to a public school in Cornwall?"

"Are you crazy? Leslie, one of my best friends is a homosexual and I love him dearly but I certainly do not wish my son to become one!"

"Good God, Sam, not all boys who attend boarding-school become homosexuals. And what about you – you went to boarding school and you're not a lesbian, *I hope*!" We both roared with laughter.

We talked and talked and finally came to the decision that we would sit down together and discuss it with Ray. After all, he was still in his formative years and we were the ones who held his future in our hands. It was not something that could be dealt with overnight in a whimsical fashion.

Ray sat and listened carefully as we laid all the alternatives at his feet. He gave me a sad look and said, "Either way I'll be separated from you, Mum."

Les and I exchanged glances. I had not realised that such strong apron strings were still attached. Was he scared of losing me? I suppose he was, really.

"Yes, we'll be separated, but not forever, and you would be with me and Uncle Les for eight weeks every year, and if you choose a public school here, you will be with us during all of your school holidays."

Ray was quiet for some time before he heaved a huge sigh and said, "I guess I would prefer to be at public school here, but do I have to give an answer now?"

"Course you don't, mate. You just take your time and think it over," said Les.

Mrs Mosham greeted us at the door when we arrived back at the flat in London. She was all excited and somewhat agitated.

"Hello, loves. Samantha, I have an urgent message for you. Gentleman by the name of Mr Brownfield came by a couple of days ago and left this note." She handed me a small envelope.

A message from Tony? Unbelievable. I ran upstairs and ripped it open. Ray stayed downstairs with Mrs Mosham, who offered him some ice cream.

"Dear Samantha," the note read, *"Just a quick line to say I'm in London for two weeks, staying at the Regent Hotel, Piccadilly. Please call me. It's urgent. Tony."*

My heart raced. I couldn't believe Tony wanted me to contact him, especially remembering the last time I had seen him at the Chinese restaurant and how he had been so distant towards me.

I grabbed the phone and called the Regent Hotel. They put me through to Tony's room.

"Hello," said that deep, familiar voice.

"Tony? It's Sam. I just came back from a week's holiday in Cornwall and got your note."

"Yes, your landlady said you were away and were expected back in a day or two. How are you, Sam?"

"I'm fine. Just fine. And you?"

"I'm okay. Listen, I would like to talk to you in person. Would you like to have dinner with me at my hotel?"

"What, tonight? Tony, I would love to but after a long journey I'm a bit tired – plus I don't want to leave Ray – my son – with the landlady the first night we're home. Could we make it tomorrow night?"

"Sure thing. Meet me in the foyer at six thirty and we'll have a drink at the bar before eating. How's that?"

"Sounds wonderful. Tony … uhm … is Greta with you?"

"Hell, no! But we will discuss that when I see you, okay?"

"Okay. 'Bye."

"Look forward to seeing you tomorrow. 'Bye, Sam."

So, Greta was not with him. Greta was not with him last time either. Dared I hope they had split up?

I was very excited all evening and Ray kept looking at me in wonderment while we watched television. I felt I owed him an explanation.

"Ray, an old friend of mine is in London for a couple of weeks. I am going to have dinner with him tomorrow night. He is staying at an hotel in Piccadilly."

"Piccadilly! Gosh, can I come too?"

I wasn't prepared for that. "Honey, not this time. I promise I'll take you to dinner one night at a posh restaurant though. We'll go to the Savoy. How's that?"

Ray laughed. "You can't afford the Savoy, mum!"

"Well, we'll go somewhere nice. Not Lyons Corner House."

I dressed up in my glad rags the next evening. I had excitedly told Mrs Mosham all about my date and she said it was no problem, Ray could stay with her. She was glad to see me getting out. Before leaving, I went downstairs to get her approval of how I looked. I was wearing the pastel pink skirt and top, covered all over with sequins, which I had bought at the Harrods sale.

Mrs Mosham whistled. "That should knock him loopy!" she exlaimed, and my beloved son said, "You look beautiful, mum." I kissed him goodbye, grabbed my summer coat and raced out the door to catch a bus to Clapham Common Tube Station.

I'm sure I smiled my entire way to the Regent Hotel, and I didn't care if my travelling companions along the way thought I was mad.

I composed myself and behaved in a ladylike manner when I reached the hotel lobby.

I sat down in a comfortable sofa and was not there more than two minutes when Tony arrived. He looked smart and handsome in a dark suit, pale blue shirt and blue tie. He came right over and sat beside me. "You look stunning," he said.

"You don't look so bad yourself – as handsome as ever."

We went to the bar and I chose a Harveys Bristol Cream while Tony had a whisky and soda.

"Do you always stay at this hotel when you're in London?"

"I find it very handy, and central. As I told you, our firm does business with a British firm in the City, and if I have to entertain, here is as good a place as any, although John, whom you met, prefers Chinese food."

We sipped our drinks in the smoke-filled bar, which I hated, but did not wish to upset Tony by letting him know that. He must have read my thoughts, however, as he said, "Let's finish up these drinks quickly and get out of here – it's too smoky."

We went into the restaurant which was tastefully decorated. Efficient waiters with napkins over their arms flitted to and fro, and one came bouncing over to us. We ordered *hors d'ouvres*, after which we both chose the filet mignon with mushrooms.

Tony gazed across the table at me. "You're looking well, Sam. What I'd like to say to you is that I'm sorry for my behaviour the last time we met."

"You don't ..."

He held up his hand. "Let me finish. I behaved like a lout and you know it."

He took a sip of his drink. "See, I was caught off guard. I saw you there, with this black man. I knew it wasn't your husband, Albert, because ... well, because I had been told he was very light-skinned. I just did not know what to think. Then you came over and explained that it was Kellman's son and I still didn't know what to think. I was confused. Why were you with Kellman's son, and where was your husband? I was a bit miffed, but I shouldn't have shown it."

"That was perfectly natural. I realised that you had picked up the wrong vibes but there was nothing I could do about it. It would have been embarrassing, with John there, to have gone into lengthy details."

"Yeah, well. But then again, you didn't owe me any explanations. You had your life to live and you chose your path. You weren't tied to me." He leaned forward and said smilingly, "I was jealous, though!"

I laughed. He was the same old Tony. "So – what do you know about me now, Mr Brownfield?"

"Well, I know that you and Albert are divorced, and Roy gave me your address and phone number before he buzzed off to Martinique."

"And, the million dollar question – what about you and Greta?"

"Likewise divorced. We have two children, a boy and a girl. I was given custody of the children."

"What! The Courts in England would never do that – give custody to the father."

"Well, the Courts in Barbados follow the English pattern but there are extenuating circumstances. It seems they found Greta an unfit mother."

"Oh, my God. Tony, I am sorry. You don't have to give me the details."

"I know, but I wish to. Set the record straight, you know? Greta and I had a whirlwind romance, so to speak. I came home on holiday from Canada, we met up, went out twice only, and I got drunk and carried away. I proposed to her the same time. Sam, she was a sex maniac – she exploded like a bomb in bed! It was stupid of me to think of building a marriage on such a foundation but I … well, I had lost you, and I just went to pieces. She never loved me. After we were married, she went careering out nearly every night, drinking and carrying on with other men." Tony sipped his drink quickly.

"Tony, I am so sorry, really I am. Sorry about *everything*. I made a complete ass of myself, as you know. I had the hots for Albert, as they say, and I was blindly in love with him. It was only during our divorce proceedings that I realised he had just used me – he was never in love with me. I should have realised it long before, because I never felt I was ever *reaching* him, if you know what I mean. He was unfathomable and unpredictable. Sexy and passionate but remote in other ways."

"You're not still in love with him, then?"

"Absolutely not. I went through the hate stage, and then there was just numbness. I was glad to be rid of him."

"I had a word with Kellman before I left Barbados, you know. He is living in a nice little house that your father bought for him."

"I know. What did he tell you about me?"

Tony looked hurt but at the same time a little annoyed. "He said you went through hell, Sam. He said that man Albert is a maniac."

So Edson had talked. I wondered just how much he had revealed. I had told Edson everything, including how I had nearly been run down by the car with Albert and Sheila in it. Had he told his father that?

"I could kill Albert, do you know that, Sam? I could *kill* that bastard. You never even wrote home and told anyone what was happening. Not even Roy. Why did you not appeal for help?"

"Tony, I had help. Lots of it. I had some wonderful neighbours, and one in particular – Jean. She died shortly before my divorce became final, and her husband, Les, who went to live in St Ives, keeps in touch with me."

Tony leaned back in his chair. "Ah-hah – so that's what you were doing in Cornwall!"

This situation called for some tact. I took a drink of water and braced myself. "Tony, I won't lie to you. Les asked me to marry him. That guy has been stringing along, waiting on a positive answer from me. Several times I have advised him to find someone else because I am not in love with him and I was fearful that if I married him it might not work out. It would not be fair to him, and I might feel trapped. Leslie does not seem to be interested in anyone else, however. He says it's me or no one. I went to St Ives for the second time just to see how I felt when I saw him again, and even more important, to discuss Ray's future. I needed Les's advice and support."

"Ray's future? What do you mean?"

"I mean his secondary schooling. I really would like him to attend Harrison College and there would have been no problem before my parents went off to Australia because he could have lived with them – although I was worried about Wilfred's dominance over him – and I would have come back to England and gone to St Ives."

"And now?"

"Well, when I mentioned to Les that Ray could live with Kellman in Barbados and come over for the long summer holidays, he was a little skeptical. Well, you know what I mean – Kellie, the butler, sort of thing – and Les wondered if Ray would have the same standard of living to which he was accustomed."

Tony looked down at his plate and was about to say something but I continued. "I know exactly what you're thinking – that Les is right. But you don't know Kellman. He is one big snob, just like Wilfred. If anything, he would be over-protective towards Ray. You know, I had also toyed with the idea of asking Joyce, Roy's mother ..."

Tony raised his hand to stop me. He had a look on his face that was impossible to interpret. It was a mixture of guilt and fright all rolled into one. I leaned forward, the better to read his expression.

"Sam, I have to tell you something, and now is as good a time as any. It may upset the apple-cart and end our friendship. I sincerely hope not, but it must be said." He paused and I stared at him. "Sam, Albert Wetherby is my half-brother."

My hand jumped on the table and nearly knocked over the glass of water. I tried to digest these last words of Tony's, with as much difficulty as a rattlesnake trying to swallow a cow. I felt the blood draining from my face. Tony reached for my hand across the table and held it tight. "Sam, please don't hate me."

Hate him! Why should I hate Tony for what he had just revealed to me? I wanted to know the details. This was no time to hate Tony – he had done me no wrong.

"Listen, Sam, Albert's mother was a beautiful lady. She came to help in the house once when my mother was ill, and my father – well, you know he drinks heavily. He had an episode with her – it was a one-night stand – and unfortunately, Albert was the result."

I leaned back in my chair and stared at him. I think there is a word for such a situation, but it escapes me. *Touché*, is the nearest I can come to it!

"Oh, God, Sam, say something. Explode! But don't look at me like that. I wasn't responsible for the situation."

Poor Tony. He thought I was blaming him. He thought I was shocked. The truth is, I was bowled over, yes. Shocked, no. Since Barbados had been colonised, such affairs had been commonplace. I put my hand up to my mouth to stifle a giggle. What a coincidence; what a paradox! It was unbelievable.

I leaned forward and placed my hand in his. "Tony, of course you're not to blame for that situation – who would ever think you were? – and I am not shocked, but completely overwhelmed." I kept looking at him and shaking my head. "You and Albert – half-brothers!" Ah-ha – so now I understood why I had seen a similarity in their eyes so many years ago. Four liquid sexy brown eyes!

"Well, well, well! Did you actually know Albert, then?"

Tony shook his head. "No. I never met him, but our garden boy who lived in Paynes Bay used to tell me about him, so I had a rough idea what he looked like."

"Did your dad and mum know that you knew about him?"

Tony shrugged and made a face. "It was never discussed but I suspect they knew, because they knew the servants knew, and servants talk."

I smiled. "So where do we go from here?"

Tony squeezed my hand. "Wherever you wish to go, Samantha!"

We both stared at each other, leaned back in our chairs and began to laugh. Well, it was funny, if nothing else.

"Let's get back to the subject of Ray for the moment, Tony. I was saying that Les and I had talked about his schooling. Well, what Les did suggest was that we consider the possibility of a public school in or near Cornwall."

"Can I ask you one very important question?"

"Go ahead."

"Have you consulted Ray – my nephew – on the matter? He is how old now, ten, eleven?"

"He just turned ten in July this year. I have to make up my mind quickly because he will sit the Eleven Plus in May next year, I think. To answer the first part of your question, yes, Les and I talked to him. He was concerned at first because he would be separated from me for a long time, and after much thought he said he would prefer to go to boarding-school here."

Tony looked thoughtful. "Well, Sam, I can't tell you what to do. You have to make up your mind about Leslie and, of course, about Ray." He paused, cleared his throat and continued. "For my selfish part, I would like you to return to Barbados. I would, in fact, like to see more of you, but I don't know how you feel about that." He sounded sincere and he looked me directly in the eyes.

"Tony, I was married to a *coloured* man. I have a *coloured* son."

Tony looked surprised. "I can't believe I am hearing this from you. Have you forgotten so quickly that the same *coloured* man is my half-brother? And did you not tell me once that your father had mixed blood? And don't you yourself know that many so-called white Barbadians are in fact from mixed ancestry? How many of them could really claim to be 'white', as in Caucasian?"

"Yes, granted, but I stirred things up a bit more, didn't I!"

"So what! I'm surprised you would think that would bother me. I have absolutely nothing against Albert's colour, just against *him*, as a person. He's a rotten bum and you know it. But that's in the past. You have to move on. As I said, you will have to make up your mind about Les. I know what I want, and it is to be with you again, even if we have to get to know each other all over again before actually considering marriage."

"There is this little thing called 'love' to be considered, Tony."

"I still love you, Sam. Always will."

I gazed at Tony. I knew then that I loved him. Had probably loved him all along but it had got pushed into the background because of the exciting passion that I had felt for Albert. Flash, bam, alakazam. It had totally engulfed whatever feelings I had for Tony, and I had pushed them aside.

What I felt now for Tony was something solid. Not a blinding passion. A strong friendship, with the budding stage of romance lingering on the fringes, waiting to burst into full bloom. The room felt warm and cosy, and when Tony reached across the table and touched my hand, I tingled and glowed all over and remembered that night at Club Morgan when I had come close to falling in love with him. We gazed at each other for a long time, interrupted only by the waiter who had come to ask if everything was okay, and would we like some coffee or tea. I was truly happy for the first time in a very long time.

16

"Honey, you won't need that thick sweater in Barbados," I said to Ray as I watched him eagerly packing his large suitcase.

"But it's my favourite sweater."

"It takes up unnecessary space, but if you insist."

We were packing to go home – to Barbados. We were now into April 1965 and Ray's school had just broken up for the Easter holidays. Once again, Wilfred had sent a sizeable draft – five hundred pounds – and I had decided to fly over on BOAC. We had one week to go.

I had done a lot of thinking during those last few months the previous year and Tony had telephoned regularly from Barbados. We had seen each other several times since our dinner at the Regent Hotel. He had visited the flat and met Ray, and one day we all went on a Thames boat ride to Greenwich. Tony and Ray seemed to like each other but I couldn't help wondering if Ray was confused, having known Les for so long and no doubt having thought of him as a possible stepfather, and then having to adjust to this new man in his mother's life.

I was no longer in doubt as to which path I would take. I knew for sure that I was in love with Tony. It would break my heart to have to tell this to Les but it had to be done, and the sooner the better. Albert would no doubt do his nut when he found out.

The American couple had vacated Ginger Lily, so we would go straight there. It was fully furnished so I would not have the bother or expense of buying furniture. I spoke excitedly of the beach and sea to Ray and he seemed anxious to be there. His school had installed an indoor swimming pool and he had learnt to swim. He enjoyed all sports.

I sat down and wrote a long letter to Les but had to stop to dry my eyes several times. I begged him to let us remain friends and to keep in touch, and if at any time he felt like taking a holiday in Barbados, he would be most welcome to stay with us.

He surprised me by coming up to London to see us off. So too did Edson. We all met at the BOAC terminal, where we checked in and took one of their buses over to Heathrow. It made an interesting picture – Ray and I, Les and Edson. People must have wondered which one was the husband/boyfriend – the black or the white.

After my terrible experiences with Albert, Les's opinion of black West Indian men had somewhat soured, but as Ray and I boarded the bus we glanced back to see Edson and Les chatting affably. An unforgettable picture of two dear friends etched in my mind.

Mrs Mosham had been visibly upset when saying goodbye to us. She clung to Ray and said, "Now, you come back over and visit me sometime, my pet." She and I exchanged hugs and tears. She had been good to Ray and me. Her words touched me: "My Cinderella, your Prince has come. God bless, and take care."

Just before we left, I telephoned the Bowlings to say goodbye. Mrs Bowling spoke to Ray and told him not to forget her and Dad Bowling, and to write to them and send postcards from Barbados.

We had a smooth take-off, and as I looked down upon the London landscape below, becoming more obscure by the minute, I sobbed. England had offered me a safe haven from the contempt and scorn of Barbadian society which Albert and I would have had to suffer had we remained in Barbados, and after dusting off the remnants of dirt associated with my years with Albert, I had been reasonably happy.

It would have been nicer if Ray had been able to grow up with a father, of course, and who knows, if Tony had not come back into my life, I probably would have opted to live in St Ives.

I glanced at Ray. His eyes were wet and red. It was the only home he had known and now here we were, being whisked off in a big mechanical bird, I to my land of birth, and Ray to a strange new land, about which he had heard so much but had never seen. The true test would come when we settled in, in Barbados.

I had left a letter to Albert with Mrs Mosham to post for me. When he got it, we would be in Barbados. I did not mention Tony. He could not try to stop us leaving. It was very brief and to the point, simply informing him that I had decided that in the best interest of Ray's education, I was returning to Barbados, hoping to enter him into Harrison College. I had not mentioned our date of departure. I had never given him my telephone number nor Mrs Mosham's, so he would no doubt find himself on Mrs Mosham's doorstep asking for details. He would get none from her and I'm sure she would slam the door in his face!

The long flight – nine hours – was uneventful, and because of the time difference we arrived at Seawell Airport around three in the afternoon.

As we emerged from the Arrival Hall into the brilliant Barbadian sunshine, four people rushed forward to greet us – Tony, Roy, Kellman and Meg. We were overwhelmed. Roy – of all people! He had flown over from Martinique specially to welcome me back and to meet Ray. Standing a little way off but coming forward now that the rush was over, was Uncle Walter, Wilfred's brother. His wife had died, and his children, my cousins, with whom I had not been very close, were all married and away from the island – two in Canada, one in Australia and one in New Zealand. The great white mass exodus from Barbados.

There were the usual kisses and hugs all round, and Ray seemed quite excited. It was decided that Tony, Ray and I would proceed, with all the luggage, to Ginger Lily in Tony's American Chevy, and Roy, who had borrowed his mother's car, would bring Kellman and Meg, both insisting that they would get there one way or another, as they wanted to prepare an evening meal and see us settled in. Uncle Walter had to get back to work.

I gazed in fascination along the way at all the changes that had taken place in Barbados since I had left so many years previously. It was almost as new to me as it was to Ray. A tremendous amount of building was in progress – new hotels, hotel upgrades, new shops and boutiques, new stylish houses, particularly along the coastal roads. And there were tourists everywhere.

"What has caused this tremendous economic boom, Tony?"

"Don't you know? We've had a new government since 1961. The Democratic Labour Party under the superb leadership of Mr Errol Barrow. We call him 'Dipper, the Skipper'. The man is a genius."

I looked at him in amazement. "But I thought the white people were scared of him because he has turned the tables around, and they're all running to Australia and New Zealand. They are calling him a racist."

Tony laughed. "They're idiots." Then he must have realised what he had said and quickly tried to make amends. "Sorry – I know your folks went to Australia too, but believe me, Sam, it is totally unnecessary. I know Mr Barrow personally. A very strong personality with an unrivalled desire to see his people – the black people – given a better standard of living. As you travel along throughout Barbados, you will see what I mean. Gone are all the white faces in prominent positions in the banks and in the public sector, replaced by blacks. His main thrust has been education. He introduced free secondary education. He is also encouraging the manufacturing sector, opening up local industries. He has completely turned the island around. Barbados is humming, Sam."

"I have come home at the right time then."

Tony squeezed my hand. "In more ways than one."

Ray's eyes were darting from one car window to the other, taking in all the new fascinating sights.

Ginger Lily looked much the same as when I had left. The American couple had looked after the garden and the lawn was well manicured. The two pink frangipani trees at the end of the lawn were in full bloom.

The view of the sea and beach as we drove up the driveway was a sight for sore eyes. How could I have ever left the place! Sometimes you have to be away from your home for a while in order to appreciate it.

Tony helped us bring all the stuff in the house and then said he had to get back to work. He lifted my chin and gave me a tender kiss on the lips. "Phone me later on. I know you will be busy settling in so I won't come back unless there is anything you wish me to do, okay?"

I nodded. I was tired. We had been up at the crack of dawn that morning in preparation for our departure. Ray, however, was anxious to stash his stuff in his bedroom and be off down the beach. It reminded me of Gwennie and me so many years previously when we had done the same thing.

Roy, Kellie and Meg soon arrived and Kellie took over as if he had never left, ordering Meg about, and picking fresh flowers from the garden. I did not dare ask what was the longterm arrangement. I had no money to pay domestic help at the moment but it was good to be pampered. I knew that Meg would not be staying, as she had gone to a new job when my parents had left.

Roy said, "I am at your disposal, duckie. What would you have me do?"

"Roy, you are so kind. I can't tell you how much I appreciate your coming over from Martinique to welcome me back. How long are you staying? And by the way, how is Joyce?"

"Mother is fine. She suffers from arthritis and moans and groans, but otherwise she's okay. I am flying back to Martinique tomorrow. Sorry I can't stay longer but Guy and I are extremely busy just now."

"What have you named the shop in Fort-de-France?"

Roy giggled. "You're going to laugh."

"No, I won't. I promise."

"*Le Roi et Guy.*" He pronounced it the French way but when translated into English it came fairly close to 'The King and I'. I did laugh.

"You've been watching too many movies, Roy. The King and (G)uy!"

"I knew you'd laugh. It was Guy's idea."

"Actually, I think it's cute, and typical of you and Guy. I hope it's a success."

"It's a huge success so far. We get quite a few orders from Paris."

Meg interrupted to ask how Ray would like his steak done. I looked at her and it suddenly dawned on me that someone had stocked up on food items. "Meg, who bought the foodstuff?"

"Mr Tony took Kellman shopping, Miss Sam."

I might have known it. I was a bit embarrassed because neither Ray nor I were used to eating steak. The few times we had had it in London was when I took Ray out to a restaurant for a treat. "Do his steak medium-rare, Meg." God, it was good to see her again. I went and gave her a big hug.

Roy took hold of both my hands and said, "Sam, it is grand to have you back. What's more I am so happy to see you and Tony together again, and I hope something comes of it. I must dash off now, because you know how it is with mother. If I have her car, she wants it. If I don't have it, she doesn't want it. After you get settled in, we must discuss your coming to Martinique for a visit. I come over to Barbados quite often so maybe sometime when I'm over, you can come back to Fort-de-France with me." He paused and gave a mischievous smile. "*If* Tony will let you!"

Ray and I had a scrumptious dinner that night, thanks to Meg, and Ray kept babbling on about the beach, the sea and the little yellow and white ghost crabs. He was completely overwhelmed. St Ives, as beautiful as it was, could not match this. The sea, even on a hot day had been chilly and there were no crabs on the pebbled beach.

Meg went home by bus later that evening but Kellman stayed on. He had planned to sleep in the Berbice chair in the verandah but I would have none of it. I insisted he sleep in the guest room.

I lay in bed that night listening to the chirping of the crickets and tree frogs, and I was awakened bright and early next morning by the distant crowing of a rooster.

One significant feature was missing. Sandy Lane factory. There was now a luxury hotel where the sugar factory had been. I used to be able to watch from my bedroom window the usual activity surrounding a sugar factory – the lighted hoist, moving from side to side, as the spider-like grab on the end of long wires snatched up a pile of canes and swung them over to the conveyor belt where they would enter the factory, and so would begin the process of sugar manufacture. At midnight, the factory whistle would blow, signaling the end of one shift and the commencement of another.

Now I looked out of the bedroom window, closed my eyes, and I could almost smell the sweet aroma of the canes being crushed and processed. But the reality was that there was no factory, no hoist, no lights, no sound of escaping steam, and no factory whistle blowing at midnight. Just a ghastly hotel!

Kellman was up before me next morning, and was busy making me a cup of coffee. Ray was fast asleep. We went out onto the veranda and I sat down. "Sit down, Kellie. We have to talk."

It took some persuasion but finally he sat, almost as if on hot bricks, opposite me.

"Kellie, I have first to apologise to you and then I have to thank you. The apology is for how I treated you when you tried to warn me about Albert before I left Barbados. I was pigheaded – as usual. I have to thank you for your continued interest, to the point where you sent your son to make sure I was okay. In my younger and less experienced days, I would have said, 'there goes old Kellie, spying again!' Edson was like a much-needed tonic at that time. He is an ambitious young man and I know he will do well at Loughborough."

Kellman nodded. "You were young and, as you say, a bit pigheaded, but I am happy to see that your strength of character and independent spirit brought you through what must have been a terrible crisis in your life. You see, Miss Sam, I had always known that Albert was no good. He was always chasing vulgar girls who had questionable characters – one such girl was even picked up by the police for prostitution and she wasn't yet sixteen. You wouldn't have known these things because his family would not have told you. Unlike white people, black people do not openly admit these things and if you tackle them, they deny everything. It forms part of their defence, and we have some 'educated idiots' walking around Barbados blaming it, and everything else, on slavery. In some ways, your father was right, Miss Sam. Black people are unable to accept and deal with their own shortcomings and social ills so they blame everything on the white man. That is not to say that I am so brainwashed that I don't blame the white man for many indescribable things but not for *everything*. There is good and bad in all races – that's the way I see it."

His words reminded me of how Albert had done nothing but deny, deny, deny, and how Jean had remarked on it.

I changed the subject. "Kellie, you know I have to take Ray over to the farm to visit the Wetherbys. After all, they are his grandparents."

Kellman rubbed his chin and frowned. "I agree, but don't expect a warm welcome from them."

I looked at him in surprise. "Why, for heaven's sake? I was not the wrong-doer. I was the victim."

"Even so, do you think Albert would have told them that? From what I was hearing – through the grapevine – you had caused all the problems. Of course I, and other people who knew Albert, did not believe that. In fact, a Barbadian man who worked with Albert in London – a man from Holetown – wrote his sister and told her the truth and she told me. Miss Sam, the way the Wetherbys look at it – well, maybe not so much the old lady – is that you forced Albert to leave his home to go and live in England with you. The two of you should never have been together in the first place. You should never have got yourself involved with Albert, in other words. That is how they look at it."

"Is that what they thought? I know the old man was always a bit distant towards me but Mrs Wetherby was nice to me."

"Mrs Wetherby is a decent lady. Mr Wetherby is a proud but simple man. I'm going to tell you something further, Miss Sam. Had I been in the same position, I would never have encouraged a romance between yourself and Edson. You were never able to deal with colour and class differences, but you have found out the hard way that they do exist, whether you like it or not."

Kellman and I sat for about an hour, chatting and reminiscing. We were at a crossroads, so to speak. I would have given anything to have him stay permanently – not as a butler – but maybe to look after the garden, which he loved. But it wouldn't be fair on him because Wilfred had retired him and given him a home up the other end of the island and I had no money to pay him.

As if he read my thoughts, he said, "Mr Walter pays a gardener to look after the garden, you know. Your father sends him the money so you needn't worry about that. I hope you don't mind if I don't stay but I have my home to look after. I have a few chickens and sheep and a vegetable plot. I'm happy, Miss Sam. I also know that Mr Tony is going to look after you."

I got up, went over to him and kissed him on his balding head. "God bless you, Kellie.You're okay, do you know that?"

It was when I went to visit the Wetherby farm, and to Holetown, that thoughts of Albert came flooding back. I quickly shoved them away and replaced them with thoughts of Tony and what the future held for the two of us, and his two children and Ray. Our romance was growing. We had made love a few times, and whereas Albert's lovemaking was passionate, it was also selfish. Tony's lovemaking was tender and giving.

We were gearing up for a talk with all the children, before taking the plunge into marriage. Tony's son, Douglas, who was two years Ray's junior, was a pleasant, well-mannered child, who looked a lot like his father. His daughter, Charmaine, was nineteen months younger than Douglas, and – yes, with a little jealousy – I could see Greta in her.

Ray got along well with them. Be that as it may, we could not pre-judge how they would feel about Tony marrying me. Greta had remarried and gone to live in Florida and appeared to have no interest in her two children.

I had easily obtained a job as secretary to the manager of a nearby hotel, and Tony had helped me choose a good second-hand car. It was a Triumph Herald. Les would have been pleased!

Ray sat the exam for Harrison College and was admitted. He was settling in fairly well. I think he was completely overwhelmed by the drastic change from his previous life, and the intense heat in the summer months bothered him. He spent a lot of time in the sea, cooling off. I noticed that he had made friends with a black boy whose family lived north along the beach. After that episode at the Tower of London he had thankfully never mentioned the word 'wog' again. He also made friends with fishermen from Boston Bay who took him out from time to time in their fishing boats. They knew who he was.

17

Tony and I got married in early December, 1965. We had waited that long because we wanted to give the children a period of adjustment. Oddly enough, it was Charmaine who had asked her father if Ray and I could come and live with them. Tony's four bedroom house was at Pine Hill, about two miles from Bridgetown. Tony kept a speedboat called *Que Pasa* at the Yacht Club, and he took the children out in it quite often.

Tony brought Douglas and Charmaine for a swim on the Saturday, two days after Charmaine had asked her question. "We have to talk marriage," he said.

While the children were swimming, we sat and made the arrangements.

"Where would you like to go for a honeymoon?" Tony asked.

"Oh, gosh, I don't know, Tony. Let me think about it."

"Martinique?" said Tony, mischievously.

I laughed. "You wouldn't dare. Roy would want to run the show!"

"St Lucia? New York? Paris? Name it, Sam."

"Know what, Tony? I have always wanted to visit Bequia. Could we go there?"

Tony nodded. "Bequia in the Grenadines it is. Quiet and romantic."

And Bequia it was. Tiny Bequia, which could only be reached by schooner or ferry from St Vincent. The perfect honeymoon spot.

The children all stayed at Ginger Lily. Tony's parents agreed to stay with them for the month and, of course, Kellman was once again in residence to help them out. As soon as I had told him the wedding date, he made it known that he would 'take over'. He would organise everything for the wedding reception at Ginger Lily and he persuaded Meg to come and help for the occasion. "That Kellman is really something else. He's an absolute treasure." Tony remarked to me. And I thought, *you'll never know how much of a treasure.*

The wedding, though comparatively small, was a spectacular event. Tony looked so handsome I had tears in my eyes! Roy came up from Martinique to be best man. Charmaine was a flower girl while Ray and Douglas were page-boys. Tony's sister, Julie, who was married with a family, was matron of honour.

Mr and Mrs Brownfield had been a little standoffish when I first arrived back in Barbados. Mrs. Brownfield had known that Albert was her husband's son but it had been kept under wraps, as such things were in Barbados. Tony and I had a good laugh when he told me they had been concerned when they heard I was returning to Barbados because they wondered if Ray was coloured and if he had woolly hair! Had not Mr Brownfield wondered, when he seduced Mrs Wetherby and she had become pregnant, what sort of child would emerge – white, brown-skinned, kinky hair? It made me laugh when I thought about it, and wished like hell that I had been able to share these thoughts with my dear departed Jean.

Such were the social patterns in Barbados still well into the nineteen sixties.

Tony and I left everyone dancing and merry-making and spent the first night of our honeymoon at the Crane Hotel, near the airport, so that we could be off early the next morning to St Vincent and Bequia.

The little hotel in Bequia was made up of a cluster of one and two-bedroom cottages, all with names of Caribbean flora.

I stopped dead in my tracks as the housekeeper, accompanied by a garden boy with our luggage, led us to our cottage. The name, portrayed boldly in black wrought iron, was Ginger Lily.

Tony and I behaved exactly as any other honeymoon couple would. We slept so late the first morning that we nearly missed breakfast.

Tony hired a self-drive car and in just two days we had driven around and seen the entire island. We frolicked on the beach and in the sea and, magically, all my past troubles and tribulations were washed away. I was truly happy. I had to pinch myself several times to believe my good fortune. I can't begin to count the times I thanked God for his goodness to me.

We both discovered that one month is too long to spend in Bequia. It is wonderful to be able to do nothing all day but lie on a beach and cool off in the glorious Caribbean sea, and this is fine for persons who are visiting from colder climes and who will be returning to cold, unfriendly grey skies, or fog and snow, but when compared with Barbados, in terms of climate and beach scenes, Bequia was very little different.

We packed up after eighteen days and went to spend the remaining ten days or so at the Fort George Hotel in Belize, British Honduras. What a contrast.

No beach in Belize – just a swimming pool at the hotel. To find a reasonable beach, we had to take a day trip over to Ambergris Caye, just off the coast, where the sea-bathing was good with a passable beach.

There were day trips into the rain forest and we even flew in a tiny aeroplane over the border to Chetumal, Mexico, where we spent one night in a very run-down hotel, eating hot tamales for breakfast, lunch and dinner, but we didn't care – we had each other.

The honeymoon over, we flew back to Barbados, spending our last two days in Miami.

We decided that we would go to Ginger Lily first, get everything packed, gather up the children and head for Tony's house where we would live. Tony suggested I give up my job because, although he had domestic help, the children were at a critical stage in their lives. Douglas and Charmaine had a new mum, and Ray had a new dad. A great deal of adjustment was called for and we thought it in their best interest that I should be at home as much as possible.

Two evenings after we returned from our honeymoon, Tony and I were sitting on the verandah having Kellie's rum punches (Kellie had refused to leave us until we left Ginger Lily) and admiring the glowing sunset painting the sky in various shades of pink, red and orange. Mum and Dad Brownfield had returned to their home that morning.

Tony sighed. "What a gorgeous sight. I don't see anything like this from my house, Sam."

I looked at him. "Tony, I don't know how you will react to what I have to say, but … well, I was just wondering – do we *have* to live in your house? I mean, could we not stay here? There's plenty of room, and …" I stopped because the look on Tony's face froze my next words.

"By Christ – you've read my thoughts! That's the second time you've done that recently. Woman, you're a witch."

I jumped up and went to hug him. "Do you mean it? Oh gosh, could we really stay here? Oh, Tony, I adore you." I showered him with kisses.

"Hey, don't get carried away. I don't see why it shouldn't work – I can rent out my house. Thing is, what about your father – would he agree?"

"*Agree!* Tony, he would be delighted."

The children were all in the living room with their eyes glued to the television. Tony held up his hand. "Hey, kids, could I have your attention for a minute?"

Douglas made a face. "Does it have to be now, Dad? We're watching something exciting."

Tony was firm. "Yes, it has to be now." He went to the television set and turned it off.

"Samantha and I have been considering staying here to live instead of going back home to Pine Hill. How does that grab you?"

No one said anything for a few seconds. They all exchanged glances. Charmaine shrugged her shoulders and said, "Could I have my own bed and everything from my room?"

Tony stroked her head. "Sure thing, honey. Whatever you want."

Ray and Douglas said, almost together, "Okay."

They did not appear over-enthusiastic, but later, before we went to bed, we heard them discussing it among themselves and they seemed more excited. Douglas was glad about it because he loved the sea, and trips in his father's boat. Tony could bring it over and moor it in Boston Bay.

Charmaine was a little doubtful at first because her best friend, Amber, lived next door on Pine Hill, but Tony said Amber could come and spend time during the holidays with Charmaine. Ray appeared to be quite happy as he had already settled in at Ginger Lily and Kelly spoiled him.

I wrote to Wilfred and asked if we could rent Ginger Lily on a longterm basis.

Tony admitted that he had been giving considerable thought as to where we would live. He had only bought the big house on Pine Hill because Greta had insisted. She wanted to live among the expatriates and embassy diplomats. She saw herself being invited to all their lavish parties. And did that happen, I asked Tony. He laughed and said of course not!

Wilfred was thrilled. He cabled us back immediately saying of course we could stay at Ginger Lily.

Darling Ginger Lily, with all the memories. This is where Tony and I would live and build our future with our ready-made family. There were lingering memories here of Albert, yes, and when I went to Holetown I could picture him on his bicycle. But that was many years ago, and perhaps a different Samantha.

The old lady who runs the store in Holetown shook her head from side to side, clicked her tongue and said to me, "My dear, I knew it wouldn't last." I knew exactly what she meant. I just smiled and said, "*C'est la vie!*"

18

A phone call from Kellman. "Miss Sam? I have some news for you and Mr Tony."

I jumped up and down. "You've sold your little farm and ..."

"Hear me out and don't be so impatient!" An order from Kellie. "I ... er ... took a trip to Grenada recently and ... er ... met a nice lady there. After I left, we corresponded and I invited her to Barbados. We got married last week "

I could hardly contain my excitement. "Oh God, Kellie, congrats, congrats! I am so happy for you. But she had better come up to my expectations and treat you good or else I'll be on her case early."

Kellman laughed, "As if I didn't know. You will approve. You will like her."

"Well, then, bring her to visit. Can you come on Saturday morning when everyone will be home?" He agreed.

Kellie married. Fancy that! I wondered what Edson would think. Come to think of it, I wondered how Edson was getting along. He had sent me a card of congratulations on my marriage but no letter.

I was soon to find out how Edson was *not* getting along. The shock came soon after Kellie had brought his wife, Ernesta, to visit. Pleasant soul – full of smiles and laughter, with an attractive, lilting Grenadian accent. Plump – as nearly all West Indian women are – shortish, brown-skinned, full round face; not a beauty, but good looking enough. I thoroughly approved.

Six weeks or thereabouts after their visit, the phone rang. It was Ernesta and she was sobbing so much that I had difficulty understanding what she was saying. The gist of it was that Kellie had had a heart attack and was in the hospital.

Before I rushed off to the hospital, I phoned Tony at work. At first, he giggled. "Oh Christ, I knew it – sex has nearly killed old Kellman!" But when he heard the consternation in my voice, he became serious. "Okay, Sam, you go ahead to the hospital. If I can get away from here I'll join you."

Kellie was hooked up to oxygen and tubes and a monitor that kept going *beep-beep*. He smiled at me as I held his hand.

Ernesta was over by his other side, constantly wiping her eyes. It was not an act. I think she really loved Kellie.

Afterwards, Ernesta and I went out to the corridor to talk. She told me a letter had arrived from Edson. He was in trouble with the police.

"*Edson*? In trouble with the police? Impossible. Not the Edson I know."

Ernesta inclined her head. "Mrs Brownfield …"

"Ernesta, please. Just Samantha or Sam. Forget what Kellie calls me – he will never change."

Ernesta nodded. She looked down at her hands which were fidgeting with her skirt. She must be truly upset over Kellie, I thought.

"Mrs Brownfield – Samantha – Edson got into a fight in London with your ex-husband."

"*What*?" I couldn't believe what I was hearing. Edson and Albert fighting?

Ernesta put a nervous hand on my shoulder. "Listen. I couldn't make much sense out of what Denzil told me." For a moment I couldn't think who 'Denzil' was, until I remembered that it was Kellie's first name.

"Soon after he read the letter, he was in a lot of pain in his chest. He handed me the letter to read. It seems Edson met up with Albert in the bar at the West Indian Students' Centre in London, and …" she hesitated and looked at me, as if not wishing to proceed.

"And?"

"Well, Albert insulted you then pushed Edson off his bar stool. Edson lost his cool and struck Albert, who fell against a table and hurt his back. He is in hospital and is suing Edson. There is to be a court case."

This was staggering news and it left me speechless. My God, will there always be remnants of Albert – apart from Ray – lingering in my life? Would Albert never give up? Poor Edson.

I pulled myself together. "Ernesta, we have to contact Edson. He should know by now that there is such a thing as Legal Aid in Britain. Whether or not he would qualify for it, I don't know. Is he in London or Leicester, could you get the address from the letter and let me have it as soon as possible?" I hesitated, then as an afterthought said, "Ernesta, I know you've not met Edson yet, but believe me, he's a gentleman, and would not lose his cool easily."

Ernesta nodded. "If he's like his father, he must be nice."

Ernesta went back to the ward and I went directly to Cable & Wireless in Bridgetown and sent Wilfred a cable with the news of Kellie's heart attack.

The next evening, the Cable & Wireless messenger delivered a cable from Wilfred. It read: "TRANSFER KELLMAN TO PRIVATE WARD STOP FUNDS ON WAY STOP LETTER FOLLOWING LOVE DAD MUM."

In the meantime, Ernesta had called me, giving me Edson's address in Leicester. I wrote to him, more or less pouring out my soul. Why did he have to go and defend me? I wasn't worth it. I had made a huge mistake in my life and I paid for it. Please try and avoid Albert in future. He is bad news. I asked him did he have legal aid, did he have a good lawyer, did he need money or anything? Against his father's wishes, I had to tell him about his father's heart attack. I asked him to please let me know by return what he needed.

The doctors attending Kellie said he would probably be in the hospital for at least one week. Tests were being carried out. He had been transferred to a private ward. He said he was quite happy in the public ward and Mr. Wilfred should not have been bothered with his problems. He scolded me for cabling Wilfred. I ignored his pleas and told him to shut up and rest.

On the political scene, Barbados was gearing up for Independence. Final decisions had been made and the date had been set for November 30th, 1966. We had a few months to go.

There were the usual mixed feelings accompanying such an achievement. It was said that the white people of Barbados were saddened at what would be the loss of Great Britain as Mother Country. Yet, English expatriates living in Barbados seldom socialised with white Barbadians. They mostly remained in their own little cliques, and no doubt considered white Bajans 'beneath' them. White Bajans did not like that, and very often, at parties, they would poke fun at the Britishers and mimic their accents.

A very amusing incident took place one day in the lounge of the
revered Yacht Club, which was a veritable haven for expatriates.
An elderly Brit was reading his *Times* newspaper when a rather
shabbily dressed young white Bajan male passed by.

The Englishman leaned forward, lowered his newspaper and
accosted the young man. "I say! Surely you're not a member of this
Club?"

The young Bajan stopped in his tracks. He gave the Englishman
a scornful look and said, "Listen, Limey, my father is the
Commodore of this Club, so put that in your Limey pipe and
smoke it." He gave the Englishman the two finger sign, said "Up
yours" and walked away, leaving the Brit with his mouth open.

The Yacht Club has remained the last bastion of 'white dominance' according to some folk. At a meeting of the board of
directors, it is decided who may or may not join the Barbados
Yacht Club, and time and time again certain whites, desirous of
becoming members, have been black-balled at board meetings.
They were not 'up to scratch', it was said. It was accepted, by such
whites, and no fuss was made; no one bell-yached because they
had been declared 'unfit' for membership of the Yacht Club; no
one threatened to burn the joint down, or 'storm the ramparts'.
Fat lot of good it would have done them anyhow!

The same cannot be said for blacks. They fussed up if refused
membership. They felt it had been on grounds of race. But the
Yacht Club authorities maintain up to this day that their decisions
are not based on race, but rather class and background. "We're not
going to have the cook's son or daughter – regardless of what
school he or she went to – applying for and gaining membership
to this prestigious establishment, and that is that." Like everything else, things would change for the Yacht Club eventually.

All eyes were now fully on Independence. A great personal trib-
ute was paid to Sir John Stow, the British Governor who had won
the admiration of all sides during his tenure of office at a very con-
tentious time. He was invited to stay on as Barbados's first
Governor General, a rare accolade for an ex-Colonial Governor.

The spanking new Hilton Hotel was opened on November
28th. The Duke and Duchess of Kent arrived to represent Her
Majesty the Queen and hand over the instruments. Church
services of thanksgiving were held all over the island and in all

denominations. Diana Ross and the Supremes, who had been invited to attend the celebrations and give a concert, nearly wound up in the Careenage when the enthusiastic crowd got a bit out of hand at the free concert.

The rains were upon us, as usual in November, and on the evening of November 29th, the ground was saturated. A special stand had been erected at the Garrison Savannah for the VIPs, both local and overseas. The Barbados Regiment splashed through pools of water and the Band of the Royal Barbados Police Force entertained in their usual highly professional manner.

Tony and I were invited by Errol Barrow to sit in the VIP stand. Tony had joined the Barbados Flying Club and was learning to fly under the expert tutelage of Mr Barrow, who had been a pilot/navigator in the RAF in World War II. Mr Barrow owned his own light aircraft.

Close to midnight on November 29th, prayers were read by ministers of different denominations and God smiled down on all – the skies cleared and the moon shone brightly.

The moment of truth. The Union Jack was lowered. The Barbados flag flew briskly in the night breeze and the new National Anthem was heard for the first time. I happened to glance around while the Union Jack was being lowered, and witnessed a few ladies – both white and black – dabbing at their eyes with their dainty handkerchiefs. I have to admit that my tears were mixed – tears for the end of British rule – both the good and the bad of it – and great emotion for this new Independent Barbados.

Tony stood tall and proud by my side, occasionally squeezing my hand. The roar from the crowd when the Barbados flag was hoisted must have disturbed the sleep of many (if anyone was sleeping at that great moment in our history) for miles around.

'Little England' – as Barbados had affectionately been known – was now well and truly on her own. Not to worry – we still had Her Majesty Queen Elizabeth as Head of State.

As regards Kellman, he was released from the hospital one week later.

We now had to deal with Edson and his court case. Ernesta had a brother in London whom she contacted, and he, in turn, paid all the legal fees after an arrangement was made whereby Kellie would reimburse him.

As it turned out, Edson had two very strong witnesses to the incident at the West Indian Students' Centre, and others had offered their support should it be required. Apparently it was not the first time Albert had misbehaved at the Students' Centre while under the influence of too many 'corn'n'oils. The case went in Edson's favour.

Roy, driving his mother's car, presented himself at Ginger Lily one fine morning in March 1967 and announced to me without preamble, "You are going to Martinique with me." He wore a skimpy pair of French shorts, a blue sleeveless shirt and sandals on his feet.

"Roy, sit down and have a drink."

"Well, duckie, I'm not staying long," he said, dropping down into the Berbice chair, "and as soon as you check with that darling husband of yours, I'll be heading back to Bridgetown to buy your ticket."

"Oh, Roy, you don't have to do that. If Tony agrees to my going, I can get my own ticket."

"Won't hear of it. Those are my conditions – take 'em or leave 'em."

"Let's phone Tony then."

We both spoke to Tony who was just on his way to a board meeting, and we had caught him off guard so he hadn't much time to think it over.

"How long will you stay, Sam?"

I looked at Roy. "One week, Roy?"

Roy made a face. "Two." I ignored him.

"One week, Tony. Roy is leaving tomorrow. Can I go with him?"

Tony spoke to Roy. "You take good care of Sam, Roy, and no hanky-panky."

"Don't make me laugh, Tony. Hanky-panky with Sam? And have Guy chop me up?"

"You disgust me, Roy! It's only because it's you that I would agree to let Samantha go."

"I'm flattered. Ta ever so, Tony. See you soon."

Roy and I went back out to the veranda but we did not sit. Roy gulped down a cold beer and belted off down the driveway in his mother's car.

Martinique is unique. Fort-de-France is a mini Paris with traffic whizzing around in every direction, car horns blaring, bicycle bells ringing. It is gay and uninhibited. I have one problem – I speak very little French, and French people tend to give you the cold shoulder if you don't speak their language.

Roy and Guy have a charming little two-bedroom house just outside Fort-de-France, and I am quite sure they went to a lot of trouble to make the guest room as comfortable as possible.

The antique shop *Le Roi et Guy* was just darling. It was housed on the ground floor of a pale pink building with a veranda on the first floor overlooking the street. Very much in the New Orleans style with wrought iron railings all round.

Inside was tastefully decorated in pastel shades, and the first thing that grabbed you as you entered the shop was a huge painting of Napoleon hanging on the far wall. No sign of the Empress Josephine, although she was born in Martinique.

"Is that for sale?" I asked Roy.

He was shocked. "Certainly not! He is too precious. Isn't he handsome?"

I laughed. "Roy, you are just too much."

Roy and Guy closed up the shop for one day and took me driving through the thickly wooded hills of Martinique, passing through quaint little villages and over to Mont Pelee, whose violent volcanic eruption in 1902 wiped out the capital, St Pierre.

There was very little to see at Mont Pelee except for an excellent museum, and the beach was composed of black volcanic sand. Quite depressing.

Although I enjoyed my week in Martinique, I was glad to be back home. I had missed Tony and the children. Ray hugged me as if I had been away for a year. He seemed to be growing taller and more handsome every day. He was doing extremely well at school and had been placed in the second eleven cricket team. The games master informed me that he would surely be an opening batsman one day. He was a first class horseman, and when Prime Minister Errol Barrow discovered this through chatting with Tony, he invited Ray to Culloden Farm, his official residence where he kept his horses, to ride with him. Ray was beside himself with excitement the first time he went. He came back home full of glowing tributes to Errol Barrow.

Just before I went to Martinique I had visited the doctor to have a pregnancy test done. I telephoned him the day after I returned home. I was two months pregnant.

Tony was over the moon. I told him that very evening as we sat in the veranda sipping rum cocktails.

"Are you sitting comfortably?" I asked, "Then listen up." Tony had just taken a sip of his drink when I said, "I'm two months pregnant." Liquid spurted from his mouth and he almost choked. He jumped up and pulled me up with him, dancing around the veranda. When he composed himself, he said, "But you didn't tell me you were going to the doctor. And how come you're not having morning sickness?"

"I wanted to surprise you if the results were positive. If not, I would not have mentioned it. Morning sickness? A little, but nothing to fret about."

Seven months later, almost to the day, an 8 lb, 2 oz baby girl presented her screaming little self to us. Tony sent a cable to Wilfred and Ellen. Wilfred had not been well recently and in fact they were both considering moving back to Barbados.

Kellie and Ernesta were among my first visitors. Kellie had lost some weight but he looked very well indeed. Ernesta was taking good care of him.

When name-choosing time came around, Tony and I decided on the names Kathleen Kelly. When we told Roy, he remarked, "How bloody Irish can you get!" He had come over from Martinique especially to see the new arrival in the family.

Ray was thrilled with his baby sister. Although he thought of Charmaine as a sister, it made a great difference knowing that he now had a blood sister. He knew about his half-sister in England but he did not remember that he had ever met her.

For some reason best known to herself, Meg left her job, appeared at Ginger Lily about a week after I came home from the hospital, and announced that she was going to be baby Kathy's nanny. No 'ifs' or 'buts' about it. I was overjoyed to have Meg back. She was by now showing signs of middle age but was full of energy and quite capable of minding a baby.

19

WILFRED died in February 1968. He had had a massive heart attack and all attempts to revive him had failed. He and Ellen had decided to return to Barbados, and were making final preparations to travel on the P & O *Canberra*. Wilfred did not like flying. They had planned on staying with Uncle Walter before renting a small furnished apartment. They had no desire to live at Ginger Lily, they insisted.

Ellen spoke to us on the phone and told us that she was having Wilfred cremated and bringing his ashes home to Barbados. She had cancelled the booking on the *Canberra* and was flying from Sydney to Los Angeles, Miami, and on to Barbados. Gwennie would be accompanying her, and would spend three months before returning to Australia. This was great news. I was looking forward to seeing Gwennie again.

I thought a lot about Wilfred in those few weeks before Ellen and Gwennie's arrival. I was glad that we had made up our differences and were on excellent terms. I would never have forgiven myself if he had died with animosity between us. I think I began to understand him over the years, and I realised that he had a chip on his shoulder, poor old blighter, due in no small measure to the social climate of Barbados, which had of course changed considerably over the past few years under the influence of Errol Barrow and the Democratic Labour Party.

Wilfred had never been able to fully accept the fact that he had coloured blood running through his veins. He was, in fact, in self-denial. No two persons are alike, and whereas ancestry seemed not to bother Uncle Walter – for after all, you are who *you* are, and not who your ancestors were – Wilfred had never seen it in that light. This was a shame because it had plagued him all his life. One did not seek the expert advice of a psychiatrist in those days in Barbados, because it was felt that anyone who suffered from depression or melancholia was simply 'mad' – to be avoided! Ellen, in her own soft way, had been the anchor for Wilfred.

I was only sorry that I had not been able to sit down and have a heart-to-heart talk with him. Perhaps it would have helped him, perhaps not. I would never know. I pitied him, but I also loved him.

What I did manage to do, however, was to have a long chat with Ellen a few days after she and Gwennie had arrived, weary and worn out from their very long trip from Australia.

I had to tread delicately when approaching the subject. She was still very upset over Wilfred's death, and very vulnerable. She and I were sitting alone on the veranda one evening while Tony, Gwennie and the children were watching television.

"Mum, there is something I have to say to you. I could not discuss it with Dad, because, well, you know how touchy he was on certain subjects." I paused because she looked a little worried. She said, "I think I know what you wish to discuss and it's okay. Go ahead."

"I'll come straight to the point. My grandmother – did you know her?"

She nodded. "Just as I thought. The answer is yes, just for a short while. She died before you were born. You have to understand, Sam, I did not dare discuss these things with you and Gwennie because Wilfred would have been very upset." She paused. I waited. "He – oh God, Sam, he ..." She broke down and began to sob.

I got up and went and put my arms around her. "We'll say no more."

She dried her eyes and then held herself very erect. "He had a rough life as a child, as you know. It was because of the social stigma. His father marrying a coloured lady and all that. He simply could not deal with it so he just pretended it didn't exist. He had to concentrate on his father's side of the family. That was his only defence mechanism."

"I understand that now. But Mum, she was his *mother*. How could he deny her? How could he not love her?"

Ellen gave me a swift look. "You are wrong. He did love her. From what I can understand, when he was a young lad he defended her. It's just that he – well, he never talked about her."

"Have you talked to Gwennie about it?"

Ellen gave a nervous little laugh. "Gwennie is not like you, Sam. Matter of fact, she's a bit like her father. I did try to tell her certain things after he died but she shrugged it off. Didn't want to know. I still don't know why it bothers you."

"It doesn't bother me. What bothers me is that Dad could not talk about his own mother. He spoke a lot about his father; he made trips to England to visit the English la-de-da cousins; he went to Somerset House and the College of Heraldry to dig up information on his English ancestry. But we know absolutely *nothing* about his mother. That does bother me, Mum. Or rather, I should say it *did* bother me. It doesn't any more except that I just wanted to know what she was like, what she looked like."

"Well, at least you know she wasn't *black*."

"I don't give a *damn* what shade she was! Was she tall, fat, thin, good-looking, pleasant, unpleasant – these are the things I want to know."

Ellen laughed. "You really are a case, Sam. She was a fairly tall, well-built woman, with thick, jet black hair. She looked rather Hispanic, actually. She was very pleasant but rather a subdued soul. Spoke only when she was spoken to, far as I can remember."

I shook my head. "Poor soul. I'm not surprised she was subdued!"

"Sam, your father really loved his mother, if that's what you're wondering. He spoke to me – if to no one else – about her."

Gwennie appeared on the veranda with a drink in her hand. "What are you two whispering about? And who wants a drink?"

Ellen said she would have a cocktail and I settled for one too. Gwennie disappeared inside to fix the drinks.

"Well, do you feel better now?" Ellen asked me.

I nodded. "Yes. Thanks for talking about it."

Ellen spoiled baby Kathy rotten. She lulled her to sleep at night by rocking her in her arms, singing Irish ditties and cooing at her. And when Ellen wasn't spoiling her, Meg was.

Gwennie cornered me one day, as I knew she would eventually. We had gone to Bridgetown together to stroll around and do some shopping, and we ended up at the inevitable 'watering hole' – Goddard's restaurant in Broad Street with its veranda overhanging the street so that you could sit and watch the endless stream of traffic – human and vehicular.

I had a cold beer and Gwennie had a rum punch. "Hate to say this, Sam, but damn glad I don't live here. The island is as beautiful as ever, but my God, the black people – they …"

I whirled on her. "Gwennie, don't."

"Don't what?"

"Don't start on that. You sound like Wilfred. Please don't take over where he left off. You have to realise that the blacks are in the majority and whites are the minority. We have a black Prime Minister, and, I might add, Tony is very friendly with him and Ray goes horse-riding with him. He is doing great things for Barbados."

Gwennie made a face and shook her head slowly. "I understand that, Sam. It is the *mentality* of the … er … black people that I cannot fathom. Look at how they try to push you off the sidewalks; how they look at you with contempt and hatred. They weren't like that before I left home. Another thing, where are all the white people? It used to be a regular thing to come into Bridgetown and see lots of white faces and meet up friends and end up here at Goddard's for a drink. What has happened to all that?"

I laughed. "The whites? They've all done what you did. Emigrated. Gone to Australia, New Zealand, Canada and the USA. The ones who have remained here keep very much to themselves, and, yes, I have to agree they don't come into Bridgetown as often as before, partly, I suppose, because of the aggression you spoke of. There are supermarkets and small mini-marts springing up all over the place, and they do their shopping there. But, Gwennie, ten years ago, the whites were doing the exact same thing to the blacks. Don't you think it's 'payback time'?"

"Two wrongs don't make a right." She took a swig of her rum punch and immediately changed the subject. "So when are you going to visit me in Aussie?"

I laughed. "That won't be for another few years with Kathleen being so young and all. Tony and I have talked of visiting you and family, but it would be a couple of years down the road."

"That was the most sensible thing you ever did – marrying Tony."

I finished my beer and looked directly at her. "I know what you're leading up to, so let's get it over and done with. I fell madly in love with Albert Wetherby. As far as I was concerned, the sun shone through his backside; the moon through his eyes. I was utterly hooked on the guy. I wanted to spend the rest of my life with him. It didn't work out that way. Albert tricked me from beginning to end. I truly believed he loved me, but he was playing a game. It was a dangerous game but I put my trust in God and He got me out of that situation. Time heals, Gwennie, and here I am with a wonderful husband and a fine family, and I might add how happy I am to be with my sister again – all's well that ends well."

Gwennie leaned across and held my hand. "I heard you went through pure hell with Albert. I am sorry I wasn't there to help and support you. You know I was quite bitter when I heard you had married a coloured man. Yes, I suppose I take after Wilfred in that respect. Keep the family white, sort of thing."

That statement stunned me. Oh no, I couldn't let Gwennie get away with that! "White, Gwennie? *Pure white,* us – you and me? Listen, I don't want a showdown with you – we've been separated for too long, but let's get a few facts straight. You know damn well that we are not pure white. Why can't you accept that? You can't change it or just blow it away like snowflakes, and the sooner you accept it, the better."

"Sam, in case you don't know it, there are lots of other 'white' families with similar backgrounds to ours, and they do not look back. They move forward. To all intents and purposes they are *white.* Why can't *you* accept that?"

"Oh, I accept it. It's you and all those others who can't accept the *truth!* The skeletons are kept tightly locked away in cupboards and never brought to light. That is not accepting facts – that is *hiding* them!"

"Okay, let's agree to disagree and leave it at that. Can we get out of Bridgetown now? I'm dying to plunge into the sea and cool off."

Wilfred's ashes were buried in the Kinley family vault at Westbury Cemetery after a small interment service, attended by family and friends.

Gwennie went back to her tribe in Australia after what she said were three glorious months. I was sorry to see her go even though we had our occasional tiffs. I think we became closer as sisters all the same – if not physically, at least spiritually, and I learned to accept her as she was, even with her prejudices.

Uncle Walter found Ellen a beautiful little two-bedroom furnished apartment in Hastings on the south coast, not far from his home. She fell in love with it because it had a small garden with a strip of lawn, and a huge, shady pride-of-India tree under which was a white-painted wrought iron garden table and chairs, where Ellen could have her afternoon tea.

Tony and I had offered to convert Wilfred's office into a 'Granny' apartment for her but she said she did not wish to crowd us. That was typical of Ellen. She knew she would be welcome to come and spend as much time with us as she wanted, whenever she felt like it.

We decided to go ahead and convert the office anyhow. If at any time Richard and Gwennie, with their children, wanted to come over, they would have somewhere to stay.

We turned it into a small two-bedroom apartment and fixed it up with inexpensive furniture. Tourism was flourishing in Barbados. New hotels had sprung up almost overnight and older ones had been upgraded. The tourist market consisted mainly of Canadian and North American visitors. We decided to advertise the cottage for rent to visitors to the island. We built a walkway leading from the back of the cottage down to the beach so that tenants did not have to pass through our garden and in front of Ginger Lily to get to the beach. It was completely self-contained.

The cottage proved to be a valuable source of income and we met some very pleasant people, and a few not-quite-so-pleasant.

Sometime in April 1969, a letter from Leslie in St Ives took me by surprise. We had exchanged Christmas cards and Ray had written to Les a couple of times. Other than that, correspondence had been kept to a minimum. Les's letter read:

Dear Sam and Tony,

Guess what? I got married. Her name is Fiona and she is a doctor's secretary. We met at a wedding reception and the following Saturday I invited her to go to the cinema, and dancing afterwards, and we started dating from there. She is ever so good to me and helps Mum and Dad. Dad is bed-ridden now with the arthritis and needs constant attention.

Guess what again? We went to a travel agent and they showed us lots of brochures – Costa Brava, the Algarve, and all sorts of romantic places, including Barbados. It was Fiona who decided on Barbados for our honeymoon, so here we come. We are going to stay at a hotel called Coral Reef Club on the west coast. Is that near you? We hope so. We are flying over on BOAC on May 20th. Is the weather good at that time? Bound to be better than here!

Look forward to seeing you and Tony and Ray.

Best wishes from Les and Fiona.

I was overjoyed. All through the years after leaving England, I had hoped that Les would find a wife. And now they were coming to Barbados! Had they known, they could have stayed in our cottage instead of having to pay all that money for an hotel, but on the other hand, knowing Leslie as I did, I think he would have felt a little awkward doing that.

I telephoned Tony at work and gave him the news. The first thing he said was, "Couldn't we offer them the cottage?" and I replied that that thought had occurred to me, but I didn't somehow think Les would go for that idea.

As soon as Ray came home from school I told him the exciting news. He was thrilled. "Oh boy, I'll see Uncle Les again. Hope his wife is nice and not some old bag!"

"Ray!" I scolded, "You know that Uncle Les would not marry any 'old bag'. Of course she must be nice. You know your Uncle Les is very choosy."

I counted the days until May 20th when we all trundled up to the airport to meet the BOAC flight.

Les and Fiona were surprised to see us, and kisses, hugs, handshakes and congratulations were exchanged all round. Fiona was a petite, blue-eyed blonde – the very opposite of dark-haired, gypsy-featured Jean, now so long departed.

Leslie and Ray hugged each other and I saw a few tears glistening in Les's eyes. There had certainly been a bond between the two of them.

We decided to leave Les and Fiona pretty much alone to enjoy the beach and sea, but we offered to take them on an island tour, stopping for lunch at the seaside resort of Bathsheba on the rugged, hilly east coast.

They both appeared to be spellbound by the beauty of Barbados and they simply couldn't get over the constant sunshine, the white sandy beaches and the warm waters of the Caribbean Sea.

They invited Tony and me to dinner at Coral Reef Club one evening. I asked Les if he was still running the greengrocer shop.

He nodded. "Yes, I bought it over from Dad and I insisted on sending Mum into retirement. Hired a young local lad to help me. I … well, that is we – Fiona and I … did up the flat upstairs of the shop, and we live there. We do a brisk business in the summer, as you may remember. The winter is a bit dead but you do get the odd elderly couples drifting down to St Ives, seeking what little warmth there is."

Two days before Les and Fiona were due to leave, we invited them over to dinner. We had also invited Ellen to spend the week-end, and she became all choked up when she thanked Leslie for 'looking after my daughter at a most critical time in her life.' Les shifted with embarrassment in his chair. "Well, Mrs Kinley, we would have been very heartless people had we stood aside and watched what was happening to her without doing anything to help. Anyway, that's all in the past."

After dinner, while we were all sitting on the veranda, Ray went over to Les and said, "Uncle Les, could I show you something in my bedroom?"

Leslie patted his shoulder and said, "Sure thing, chum, point the way." They went inside the house. I wondered what Ray had to show Leslie, but knowing Ray as I did, I felt it was an excuse to talk to Leslie by himself.

And that was exactly what it was. Ray approached me the day after Les and Fiona returned to England. "Mum, I don't know how to say this because I'm not too good at words and stuff, but do you think it would be possible for me to finish off school in England?"

Now that was a shocker if ever there was one! Never can tell how children's brains work.

"Is that what you discussed with Uncle Les when you took him to the bedroom?"

He looked sheepish, and hung his head. "Yes."

I went to him and put my arms around him. "Ray, honey, are you unhappy here in Barbados?"

"Oh, no, mum. No." He was adamant. "Mum, Douglas and I talk a lot. We talk about England. We went to the Library and got some information on English public schools and all that they have to offer, especially in the line of sports."

I interrupted. "Ray, are you saying that you *and* Douglas would like to go to a boarding-school in England?"

"Uh-huh. We talked about it, yes. Remember before we left London, one of the options open to me was to attend a boarding-school in Somerset where I could stay with Uncle Les during the holidays?"

"Yes, I remember. But I got the impression that you weren't too keen on that idea."

Ray nodded. "I was sorta tied to your apron strings at that time, mum. I heard you tell Uncle Les that. Plus, I couldn't bear the thought of being away from you."

I hugged this charming son of mine. "And now?"

He wriggled. "Well, I love you with all my heart, mum, but I do not particularly like Harrison College. Neither does Douglas."

"Well, you'll have to let Doug speak for himself. Now, this calls for a family conference and as soon as Tony gets home, we'll all have a little heart-to-heart talk. How's that?"

"You mean you will consider it?"

"That's what I said." He smiled and turned away. I grabbed him back. "Give your old mum another hug, you rascal. If you're going to be leaving my apron strings, I want a lot of hugs and kisses from you from now on."

Tony was as surprised as I had been when, after dinner that night, we sat down to have a chat. Charmaine was excused because she wasn't directly involved, and she wanted to watch her favourite television programme.

Tony addressed both boys. "Is this for real, kids? You wish to leave this beautiful sunny island for cold, forbidding England?"

Ray and Douglas exchanged glances. Douglas was the first to speak. "Dad, Ray has the edge on me – he has known England and he knows Barbados. I only know Barbados. I love swimming, tennis, and boating, but I don't like school. At least not Harrison College."

"What don't you like about Harrison College?"

The two boys exchanged glances again, but before Douglas could answer, Tony cut in, "Have you been flogged by the headmaster? And if so, why wasn't I informed?"

Douglas shook his head. "I have not been flogged. Came a bit near to it once though."

Ray took over. "We don't like some of the masters – they're weird."

"*Weird?* In what way?" asked Tony.

Ray took the bull by the horns. "They're bullies. Unfair. Furthermore, the white ones are prejudiced. And …" He looked down at his feet.

"Yes?" Tony and I asked together.

"So are the white boys."

Tony sat back in his chair, stared at the two boys and pondered on this new untimely situation. I think he was wondering the same thing I was wondering. Had Ray been teased about his coloured father? Was this what was bothering them?

"But surely the white boys don't give you any hassles?" Tony looked at both boys.

They both replied together, "No. Not us!"

"Well, who, then?"

Douglas spoke up. "Dad, Ray and I have black buddies at school. They are real nice guys, and during breaks we hang out with them. We have white friends too, but, see, the white guys, when they see us with the black ones, they back off and go play somewhere else and call us names." They exchanged glances.

I didn't know about Tony but I got the picture – clearly. Oh boy, it was back to square one. The ugly prejudice. Should I have been surprised? The more things change the more they remain the same.

Tony scratched his head and sighed. "Oh, Lord. This is a hell of a situation. Where do we go from here? It's all very well to say we'll pack you up and send you off to school in England, but one thing you don't seem to realise is that at a public school in England, it is very unlikely that you will meet black boys. Maybe the son of an African chief, or an Indian or Pakistani, and perhaps none at all. What I am trying to say is that you will still be isolated. You will be strictly among white English boys. If that doesn't bother you, and you consider that because of the many other benefits you would be happier, then I guess we could consider it. Personally, I would prefer that you battle it out at Harrison College and thumb your noses at the prejudiced white boys. Do your own thing and be friendly with whom you wish. Don't let them intimidate you." Tony shrugged and spread his hands in a gesture of resignation.

"It's your choice, kids. I'll back you, but I think we should give it a great deal of consideration before taking the plunge."

I looked at Tony and then at the boys. "Where would you stay during the short holidays? Do you think we could impose on Les and Fiona? Before Les was married it would have been no problem, but it's two of them now."

"Oh, I asked Uncle Les all that and he had no hesitation in agreeing, but he said I should discuss it thoroughly with you and Tony first and then we could take it from there."

"Tell you what," said Tony, "Sleep on it, and we'll have another chat in a day or two, weigh all the pros and cons and then make a decision, okay?"

Both boys nodded their agreement.

Ellen made a very interesting comment when we told her of our dilemma. "Know what your father would say if he were alive? He would say you can't legislate people's feelings. You can wipe out practised racism but you can't stop prejudice. There are black boys from very cultured families attending Harrison College, but do you think they will associate with the fisherman's son? So, on the one hand, you have colour prejudice, and on the other, you have class prejudice, and that will never change, I don't care how many Errol Barrows you bring."

Some speech for Ellen. She of course was all in favour of Ray and Douglas going off to school in England. "Forget all the colour and class talk, it will make gentlemen of them. They will learn discipline and responsibility, attain high standards, and when they go out into the world, they will be full of self-confidence."

"Yeah. Full of class prejudice too," I piped up. Everyone ignored me.

20

B Y the end of June, the school issue had been decided. We had talked it over in detail, weighed all the pros and cons, and of course a few of Ray's and Douglas's friends had cruelly suggested that they would turn into homosexuals. But the decision rested. Ray and Douglas would enter a public school in Somerset, starting in the September term.

Tony and I would travel to England with them to see them settled in, while Ellen would stay at Ginger Lily with Charmaine and baby Kathleen. Meg would be there to help her.

Back to Blighty again! We stayed at a hotel in Bath and then took the train over to the small village near the school, and a taxi from there to the school.

Both boys put on a brave front when good-bye time came. We had met the headmaster, who seemed a pleasant middle-aged man. He lived, with his wife, in a cottage in the vast grounds. Tony nudged me and whispered wickedly, "I'm glad he has a wife!"

Ray hugged me for a long moment. "I love you, Mum, and I will miss you. And …" he hesitated.

"Yes? And?"

"Well, if we don't like it, can we use the other option?"

"You mean come back to Barbados and Harrison College?"

He nodded. "I mean, just *if* – you know?"

I hugged him. "Won't be that long, kiddo, we'll be seeing you at Christmas time and you'll get to fly to Barbados by yourselves, like two grown-up men."

Douglas hugged me too and surprised me when he said, "I'll miss you, Sam. You're my real mum!"

As the taxi taking us back to the train station moved off, I broke down and sobbed on Tony's shoulder. He put his arms around me. "They'll be okay. They're big boys now. Don't fret. In no time it will be Christmas." His voice cracked.

It was good to get back to Ginger Lily. Autumn had set in in England, with leaves on some trees beginning to turn red. All very beautiful but chilly for September.

I had a few disturbing thoughts that somehow Albert would find out that Ray was back in England but we had taken the precaution of informing the Headmaster about the situation and he had promised that Ray would get full protection.

Sometime in July, I had taken Ray over to the Wetherby Farm so that he could see his grandparents before leaving for England, but we had not told them he was leaving the island. I did not dare take that chance because, although Mr Wetherby had been his usual 'distant' self, the old lady had been a little chilly towards me. Tony said he thought it was because I had married him – Albert's half brother, and she no doubt felt bitter.

She did, however, drop a bombshell. We were in her kitchen and she had offered me a cup of coffee. I was sitting at the kitchen table sipping it when she turned away from the sink, wiped her hands on her apron, and said, "Albert and his family are hoping to return to Barbados to live next year. He has never been happy in England, you know."

I all but choked on the dregs in the coffee cup. Oh boy, was she ever piling it on me – '*he has never been happy in England – thanks to you!*' I'm sure that's what she had meant to say. Thank God, Ray had not been in the kitchen at the time. He had gone with his granddad to look at the sheep.

His *family?* Did the old lady mean Sheila and the child, or were there more children? I had no intention of enquiring, but it was rather strange the way she had stressed the word 'family'. I wondered if she were trying to impress me with the fact that Albert was now settled and happy with a family. '*You did the dirty on him, but he's happy now*' sort of thing. I truly believe she thought that I had been at fault, and I had no intention of discussing the truth of the matter. It was all dirty water under the bridge and in the past. I was sorry she felt that way about me.

Ray and I walked back home down the beach and I was so silent that Ray quickened his pace, turned around, stopped in his tracks and faced me. "What's up, mum? Something upset you?"

Oh yes, something had upset me all right – the thought of Albert coming back to Barbados. He and his family would probably live on the farm and that was too close for comfort. If he had decided to let bygones be bygones, fine. I had difficulty believing that Albert would have changed that much. And how would he react when he discovered that Ray had been sent off to boarding-school in England?

I started to run. "Beat you to the house!" I said to Ray, hoping that he would forget whatever expression he had seen on my face. We ran up to the house. Did I think I had a snowball's chance in hell of beating that athletic, lithesome young son of mine? Some hope.

Christmas was fast approaching. Kathy was now just over two years, running all over the place and getting into mischief. I swore she was too much for Meg to handle but Meg adored her.

Ellen was the next one to knock the breath out of us. She had become friendly with an old gent whom she met while sitting on a bench at the Hastings Rocks, a small esplanade with a bandstand where the Royal Barbados Police Band often performed, situated between the Hotel Royal-on-Sea, and the Hastings Hotel. Many of the elderly inhabitants of the Hastings area congregated at The Rocks on evenings to shoot the breeze.

More whites lived on the south coast, and particularly the Hastings area, than any other part of Barbados. Why this was so was a puzzle, but no doubt the sociologists could work that one out. The 'plantation' whites of course lived on the inland plantations, and the west coast whites were scattered far and few between. Perhaps it was for this reason that Wilfred had chosen the west coast, which had become very fashionable as a domain for expatriates and other foreigners. One such person was Sir Edward Cunard, the Cunard shipping magnate. He had a home on a west coast beach surrounded by at least six acres of land, all planted in flowering trees and shrubs.

It is possible that Wilfred felt that he would be more accepted among these white foreigners than among some white Barbadians, although it is true to say that since the 1950s the stigma that had been attached to persons with even the vaguest connections to 'colour' had dissolved, and into the 'white' melting pot went anyone with a white skin, regardless of background.

As regards class, well that was an entirely different matter. Class structure remained much the same and there were little cliques scattered around the island, and certain folks did not get invited to certain other folks' cocktail and dinner parties. It is very doubtful that that situation will ever change in Barbados.

Ellen and seventy-year old Mr Pitman did more than shoot the breeze. They gazed into each other's eyes and decided that they liked each other a whole heap. He was a widower and she a widow. She drove him over to Ginger Lily one Sunday afternoon and announced to us that they were getting hitched. I was shocked and thrilled at the same time. Fancy staid old Ellen getting married again. I wondered how Gwennie would take the news.

They are getting married sometime after Christmas. Tony, Charmaine, Kathy and I are at the airport, awaiting the arrival of the BOAC flight from London with Ray and Douglas aboard.

Ellen is coming to stay in the guest room and Mr Pitman will stay, with all due propriety, in the cottage.

Kellman is coming to do his butlering act – at his insistence – waiting at the huge twenty-seater mahogany table on Christmas night.

All in all, it should be a wonderful Christmas at Ginger Lily!